WED OR ALIVE

AN ANNABELLE ARCHER WEDDING PLANNER COZY MYSTERY

LAURA DURHAM

BROADMOOR BOOKS

The Wedding Ceremony of
Veronica Elizabeth Hamilton
and
Tad Alexander Donnelly

Bridal Party

PARENTS OF THE BRIDE	MR. STEPHEN & MRS. DEBORAH HAMILTON
PARENTS OF THE GROOM	MR. WILLIAM AND MRS. NANCY DONNELLY
BRIDE'S GRANDMOTHER	MRS. CANDACE MARTIN
MAID OF HONOR	VALERIE HAMILTON, SISTER OF THE BRIDE
BEST MAN	VICTOR HAMILTON, BROTHER OF THE BRIDE
BRIDESMAIDS	CARA MARTIN, COUSIN OF THE BRIDE STEPHANIE THOMAS, FRIEND OF THE BRIDE MELISSA PACE, FRIEND OF THE BRIDE KRISTEN NELSON, FRIEND OF THE BRIDE EMMA WATSON, FRIEND OF THE BRIDE
GROOMSMEN	JON GRAHAM, FRIEND OF THE GROOM TIMOTHY HARPER, COUSIN OF THE GROOM BENJAMIN ROBERTS, FRIEND OF THE GROOM PETER JOHNSON, FRIEND OF THE COUPLE GEORGE WILSON, FRIEND OF THE GROOM
READER	MS. CONNIE MARTIN, AUNT OF THE BRIDE

CHAPTER 1

$\mathcal{I}$ stood underneath the high-peaked tent and gazed past the rows of wooden folding chairs to the lush, green lawn with a barn in the distance. The massive house—built to resemble a Tuscan villa—sat at the top of the grassy slope, a long pool stretching out from its patio adorned with a statue of a Roman goddess at the far end. The white marble goddess already wore a floral wreath, evidence that my floral team had begun the pool area decor. I took my wedding day schedule from the pocket of my black dress and checked that off the timeline.

"So much for a mild summer," I muttered, tucking a long strand of auburn hair back into my bun and raising my face to one of the fans tucked high in the corners of the tent. The warm air barely stirred from ten feet overhead. I would need to turn the fans to high before the two hundred plus wedding guests arrived and filled the tent. Even though the ceremony programs were printed on fans, I suspected they would be little help in the June heat.

I glanced at one of the white, frilly programs already placed on the ceremony chairs facedown so the fanned-out feathered back was the first thing the guests would see. I didn't want to think back to how

1

long it had taken me to find feathered fans to go with the wedding
theme. Another reminder of why I hated planning themed weddings.

Since Washington, DC was a city known for understated and
classic—people wanted to spend money without it seeming like they
spent money—the closest my couples usually got to a theme was
coordinating colors and perhaps syncing the cake and the favors.
This bride and groom, on the other hand, had gone with the concept
that "more is more" in insisting we recreate Carnival in Venice at the
bride's family's home outside the city. We'd left "over the top" in the
rearview mirror long ago, and at this point I felt grateful the bride
hadn't insisted on dredging her own Grand Canal in the backyard.

Two black-and-white-clad figures waddled toward me from the
house, their arms flapping at their sides—to help them keep their
balance—and their heads bobbing back and forth. I glanced down at
my timeline again and put a check mark next to the line that read,
"Penguins arrive."

"Down here." I waved my arms in the air so the handler could see
me as I stepped out from under the tent to meet her, squinting in the
bright sunlight.

The penguins came to a stop in front of me, and I fought the urge
to pet them, reminding myself these were wild animals even though
they looked adorable. They were also the one element that wasn't
Venetian, but since the bride had collected penguins since she was a
little girl, it had been on her "must-have" list, despite my protests that
wild Antarctic creatures were a bad idea on a wedding day.

"I'm Annabelle Archer with Wedding Belles. The wedding planner." I extended my hand to the short-haired woman accompanying
the penguins. "I think we spoke on the phone."

The woman wiped her hands on the front of her gray cargo pants
and shook my hand. "I know I'm a little early, but I wanted to give
myself time to find this place."

"It's a bit outside the city." I cast my eyes over the sprawling estate
with its wrought iron gate, stately driveway lined with tall Italian
cypress trees, and horse stables complete with rolling fields. It even
smelled like we were far away from the city with the scent of cut

2

grass—and the faintest trace of horse manure—in the air. "But look at the upside. There's tons of free parking."

She chuckled. "True. It's better than hunting for a space in DC."

"The bride decided against having the penguins carry the rings down the aisle." I didn't mention that I'd spent hours talking her out of this. After a bad experience with a pair of dogs running off with the wedding rings, I'd adopted a "no animals carrying expensive jewelry" policy.

"So just the photo shoot with the couple and mingling during cocktail hour?"

"You got it. We still have a couple of hours until go time, so why don't you hang out in the house?" As if they heard me, the penguins turned and started waddling away. "I doubt your little guys like the heat."

"I think they're heading for the pool."

I personally didn't have a problem with the penguins taking a dip. "It's salt water. I think it's safe."

My assistant, Kate, did a double take as she passed the penguins on her way down the hill, stumbling a bit in her heels and catching herself before she tumbled the rest of the way.

"I forgot about the penguins," she said when she reached me.

I tapped my schedule.

"I know, I know." She flicked a hand through her blond bob. "I didn't have time to memorize it yet, Herr Commandant."

"Another date with the naval officer?" I asked, ducking back under the tent to avoid the sun.

She frowned. "He's been deployed. No, last night's date was with a lawyer who works at Langley."

I tucked my schedule back into my pocket. "He's a lawyer for the CIA?"

She put a finger to her lips and shot a glance over her shoulder. "I can't talk about it."

"You know he isn't a spy, right?" I said. "They don't send lawyers to infiltrate terrorist cells."

"We don't know that. What would be more of a surprise than a bunch of buttoned-up lawyers busting out the spy moves?" She leaned with one hand on my arm as she stepped out of her heels and wiggled her toes.

"Not much," I admitted, refraining from making a comment about the impracticality of wearing high heels to set up a wedding since I knew it would fall on deaf ears.

"Enough about my dating life." Kate nudged me. "I want to hear if there's any movement on yours."

I hoped the flush of my cheeks from the heat hid the blush I felt at the mention of my love life. After a rocky start and a bit of on-again, off-again action, I'd been seeing DC police detective Mike Reese steadily for several months. Things still weren't smooth sailing since we both had crazy work schedules—especially since I was in the thick of my busy season—and not all my friends were as crazy about Reese as Kate was. My best friend, Richard, had been giving the relationship the cold shoulder since he'd decided my dating Reese meant I spent less time with him.

"Fine," I said. "Everything's fine."

"Fine?" Kate reached into the pocket of her short, black sheath dress and produced a small cellophane bag of gummy bears. "That tells me nothing. Have you decided yet?"

I avoided her eyes. "I've been too busy to give it much thought."

"If a smoking-hot cop asked me to move in together, I wouldn't take a month to tell him yes." She held the candy bag out to me, then shook a couple into my outstretched palm. Kate kept her energy up on wedding days by eating gummy bears and analyzing both of our dating lives.

"It's complicated," I said, popping a squishy orange bear in my mouth and savoring the rush of sweetness.

She tilted her head at me. "You mean Richard?"

"And work. We *have* been busy."

Kate tossed a few gummies in her mouth, then put the bag back in her pocket. "Unless Richard plans to keep you warm at night, I don't think he should have a vote. This is your life after all."

4

"I know, but Richard has been my best friend since I moved to DC. It's hard to see this coming between us."

"He'll get over it," Kate said "He may fast in protest for a while—or maybe cut out truffle fries—but he'll survive."

My hesitation had to do with more than my best friend, but it was hard to admit I was just as afraid of my life changing as Richard. I cleared my throat. "How's the bride doing upstairs?"

"Good. She's a little nervous, so Fern's calming her down with his patented blend of charm and dirty jokes."

"As long as he's not getting the bridal party drunk," I said.

Kate hesitated. "Would you be fine with tipsy?"

I let out a deep sigh. "Are we talking him or the bride?"

Kate bobbled her head, which I did not take as a good sign.

"Hallelujah." She threw her arms in the air as she spotted the lemonade station on the other side of the tent. "I'm dying of thirst. The only thing to drink in the house is champagne." She held up a hand before I could speak. "And you know I follow your rule about not drinking alcohol at weddings."

I followed her over to the long table with the two large glass beverage dispensers, one filled with traditional lemonade and one filled with raspberry lemonade—indicated by gilded signs hanging around the glass from sheer black ribbon.

"I thought the signature drink was a Bellini," she said.

"It is, but I changed this station to lemonade. Do we really want guests getting drunk *before* the ceremony?"

"Touché." Kate took a champagne flute, filled it with plain lemonade, and handed it to me before filling her own. "No Mason jars?" she teased, knowing my aversion to the rustic wedding trend.

"Not on my watch." I took a sip and felt several degrees cooler as I swallowed the sweet drink.

"As I suspected," Richard said as he strode down the hill toward us, his beige blazer flapping. "You two are drinking on the job while I'm slaving away in the kitchen."

Kate downed her glass and refilled it. "How is it you never break a sweat when you slave away?"

I'd often wondered the same thing. Richard, owner of the renowned Richard Gerard Catering company and my best friend, had a talent for remaining spotless no matter the temperature or disaster.

"It's a lot of work to direct my staff and manage the load-in." Richard smoothed the front of his linen-blend jacket when he reached us. "Simply because I don't personally haul boxes does not mean I'm not working hard." He took out a small mister and sprayed his face with—from what I could determine from the few drops that flew into my face—rose water, then patted himself dry with a linen handkerchief and flicked a hand through his dark, spiky hair.

"Of course it doesn't." I touched a hand to his arm, hoping to mollify him. We didn't need Richard worked up this early in an event. "Would you like some lemonade?"

He eyed the glass jars. "Perhaps a drop. The sun is relentless."

June in the Washington, DC area could be mild or it could be sweltering. Unfortunately, on this wedding day we'd drawn the short straw.

Kate handed him a glass. "Bottoms up, sweetheart."

Richard took a sip and dabbed his mouth. "So refreshing." He set the glass on the table and put one hand on his hip. "You didn't mention we were having an armed militia attend the wedding."

"What?" I blinked at him a few times before snapping my fingers. "You mean the father of the bride's personal security detail?"

Richard pointed to a man in all black pacing the perimeter of the patio. "There are at least half a dozen of these guys, and they're all packing serious heat."

Kate winked at him. "You sound so butch when you talk like that."

Richard ignored her. "Isn't this excessive for a guy who owns a pharmaceutical company?"

"It's not just any pharma company." I dropped my voice. "They got a major contract with DOD last year. Very hush-hush."

"Department of Defense?" Kate asked. "What does a drug manufacturing company have to do with defense?"

I wasn't surprised Kate knew the acronym off the top of her head.

She'd dated men at every major government department and knew all the abbreviations by heart.

"And how do you know this?" Richard asked.

"You told me I should Google my clients."

Richard beamed at me. "Look at you doing research on your clients. I'm so proud. I hope you charged them more when you found out."

I headed out of the tent, gesturing for Richard and Kate to follow me. "You know I don't raise my prices because someone is wealthy."

He let out an exasperated breath. "Still so much to learn, darling."

"Anyway," I said, letting Kate lean on me as we trudged up the hill and her heels got stuck in the grass, "I figure what he's manufacturing must be top secret and pretty deadly. Why else would he have guards following him everywhere? You don't do that if you're manufacturing ADD meds."

Richard paled under his bronzer. "That's a scary thought. You don't think we're in danger, do you?"

"Kate and I have been coming to the house for six months, and we've never seen anything out of the ordinary, right?" I stepped onto the paving stones of the pool deck and waited for Kate to pull her shoes out of the ground.

She scrunched her mouth to one side. "I do see a pair of penguins swimming in the pool."

Richard held up his palms as we watched the pair of animals splash in the water. "Don't get me started on the penguins. You know my feelings on livestock at weddings, Annabelle."

"Penguins are hardly livestock. You should be grateful I talked them out of the llamas."

"Llamas? They must be out of their minds." Richard looked heavenward. "I used to think it was absurd to have dogs in weddings. Now I long for the days when a cocker spaniel was the worst of our worries."

I stepped back as one of the penguins slapped his flipper, sending droplets of water onto the pool deck.

"Watch it," Richard called out to the penguin, pointing to his shoes. "These are suede."

"I don't think he heard you," Kate said. "He's underwater."

"There you are." Fern stepped out one of the French doors to the house. "I need a little assistance."

His dark hair was pulled into a tight man bun at the top of his head, but it was the crease between his eyebrows I noticed. "What's wrong? Please tell me another bride isn't passed out cold."

"Of course not," Fern said, as if this had never happened to him before. "But she says to cancel the wedding and send everyone home. She doesn't want to get married anymore."

CHAPTER 2

"*N*ot this again." I rubbed a palm across my forehead. We'd had to deal with a groom with cold feet—who also could not stop nervously washing his hands—at our last wedding. Luckily for that bride, we'd managed to talk her intended off the ledge and convince him to go through with the ceremony before he buffed the skin off his hands.

Fern joined us on the pool deck.

"Why are you in prison stripes?" Richard asked, sizing up Fern's outfit with his arms crossed.

Fern touched a hand to his black-and-white-striped T-shirt. "These are hardly prison stripes, sweetie." He pointed to the red sash around the waistband of his black pants and the matching scarf knotted at his neck. "I'll have you know this is what Venetian gondoliers wear."

Fern considered it an art form to coordinate with the theme of the wedding, and today's wedding was indeed inspired by the couple's love of Venice. It hadn't been a stretch to plan a wedding themed around the Italian city when the bride's home—and the setting for the at-home wedding—was built to look like an Italian villa.

"I'm a little surprised you aren't wearing a carnival mask." I was referring to the ornately adorned and often gilded masks worn during Carnival in Venice and which we were using as part of the table decor for the reception.

Fern winked at me. "I have one of those and a black velvet cape to change into later."

"If there is a later," I said. "Do you think the bride is serious about canceling the wedding?"

"Who knows with Veronica and her moods? That's why I came to get you. You might have more luck talking to her. You know my patience wears thin when it comes to drama."

I eyed his themed costume and decided not to point out the obvious.

Richard fanned himself with one hand. "If no one gets to see the sugar carnival masks my pastry chef created for the individual crème brûlées, I'm going to lose my mind."

"That's not going to happen," I said. "Wedding Belles has never had a runaway bride or groom, and we're not about to start. Right, Kate?"

Kate gave me a mock salute; Richard began breathing rapidly; and Fern's eyes brightened as he spotted the penguins in the pool.

"Will you look at that?" He pointed to the black-and-white animals as they frolicked in the water. "We match!"

"Well, they don't go with my entertainment theme." A diminutive man in a navy suit strode across the pool deck, rapping his knuckles against his clipboard as he approached. "I spent months assembling a team of Venetian-inspired performers to mentally transport the guests to Carnival, and you throw penguins in the mix?" He touched a finger to his headset earpiece. "Harlequin One, do you copy?"

"Hi, Sidney Allen," Kate said, the irritation dripping from her voice. "Look, Annabelle, it's Sidney Allen."

It was never just Sidney, always Sidney Allen, and I honestly didn't know if it was his first and last name or his first and middle. Since he had a thick Southern accent and hailed from Charleston, I assumed it was the latter, and like Cher or Madonna, he didn't use a last name.

Sidney Allen was the owner of DC's top specialty entertainment firm. He was known for his "Cirque du Soleil "style troupes, his Broadway-trained actors, and his trademark headset that I suspected he wore even when he slept. Even more well-known was his reputation for being a perfectionist who drove everyone crazy with his micromanaging.

Sidney Allen didn't quite reach my shoulder and was built like Humpty Dumpty, with no discernible waist and his suit pants pulled up so high that his belt looked like it was looped around his chest. Over the years I'd known him, he'd hoisted his pants higher as his waist had grown larger. Now his hemlines barely skimmed his ankles.

"For the love of God," Richard whispered to me, "his pants are eating him."

"It's an Empire waist," Fern said in a low voice.

Richard gave Fern a withering look. "Pants aren't supposed to be Empire waist—especially not on older men."

"High waist is in, right?" Kate asked.

Fern shook his head. "Not *that* high, sweetie."

I elbowed Richard and Fern, hoping Sidney Allen hadn't heard them. The last thing I needed was a face-off between three divas.

"I didn't know you'd be on-site so early," I said. Truth be told, I'd hoped for a little more time without the diva-wrangling prima donna.

He fluttered his clipboard-free hand in the air. "If my performers are here, I'm here. I've got so many performers on-site for this wedding, I've had to divide them into teams based on the Venetian masks they're wearing." He pursed his lips. "All my Pulcinellas are here, but I'm still missing one Scaramouche." He pressed a finger to his earpiece. "Scaramouche Three? Come in, Scaramouche Three." We waited for a beat. "No. Not here."

"That's what I love about you," I said, forcing my sweetest smile, "your dedication to your clients. Don't we always say how dedicated Sidney Allen is to his clients, Kate?"

"That's one thing we say," Kate mumbled.

Sidney Allen's eye flicked to Kate then away again. "Now about these penguins."

"The penguins were all the bride," I said. I didn't like to throw my clients under the bus, but the reality was that the bride had insisted on the penguins, and nothing I said would have talked her out of them. "She's collected penguins since she was a child."

Sidney Allen cut his eyes to the animals frolicking in the pool. "It's ridiculous. There are no penguins in Venice."

"Give climate change a few more years and there will be," Richard said, bestowing an arch smile on Sidney Allen.

Fern giggled. "Won't that be a sight to see?"

The entertainment guru huffed. "How am I supposed to work this into my narrative? Every other element of this performance has been painstakingly coordinated so that it's not only historically accurate but also creates the illusion of actually being in Venice for Carnival." He stamped one foot on the ground. "Penguins destroy that illusion."

Fern adjusted his red sash. "You could always put them in masks. Then no one would know they're penguins. People would think they're short little waiters."

Sidney Allen gave him a disdainful glance while Kate put a hand over her mouth to muffle her laughter.

"Bite your tongue if you think I'd hire waiters that short." Richard put a hand to his heart. "You know I have an unspoken rule about how my waiters look."

"You assemble your team of waiters like they assemble the Rockettes," Kate said. "No one can be too short, too tall, too plump, or too homely."

Richard looked around him. "I wouldn't put it like that."

"You mean because the Department of Labor would come after you?" I said.

"That's why it's called an unspoken rule, darling," Richard said. "I like my team to have a cohesive look. Is that so wrong?"

I didn't have time to go into the legal implications of Richard's waiters being able to rival the Radio City Music Hall kickline for symmetry.

"I'm really sorry," I said, turning to Sidney Allen. "But the bride wanted penguins. If she's happy, I'm happy."

"Right now she isn't happy," Fern reminded me.

Sidney Allen's eyes popped open. "What? Why isn't the bride happy? Is it because I had to use my second choice doge?"

"It has nothing to do with your doge," I said. "Actually, I don't know why she's unhappy. Probably cold feet."

Sidney Allen hiked his pants higher. "If you ask me, brides have been given a free pass to be overly dramatic. Being engaged does not mean everything gets end-of-the-world status."

I tended to agree with him, but found it odd that an entertainment designer would complain about too much drama.

Sidney Allen screeched as a row of figures in crimson capes, shiny white masks, and velvet caps processed around the corner of the house and into the reception tent.

We all jumped, and Fern reached for Kate's arm, his mouth dropping open. "It's like a procession of grim reapers."

"Those are my performers for the path of masks," Sidney Allen said. "But what on earth are they thinking? Those hats aren't to be worn to the side. They aren't berets."

He hoisted his pants to his armpits and stalked off, presumably to reorient the hats.

"You don't think he'd let me have one of those hats do you?" Fern asked. "It would look divine with my black cape for later tonight."

"Can we please focus on the problem at hand?" I asked. "We cannot have our bride call off the wedding. Not after all this work."

"It wouldn't be ideal," Kate said. "But it wouldn't be the worst thing that's happened to us at a wedding."

"At least no one has been murdered," Fern said in a stage whisper.

Richard gave a small squeak and turned toward the dinner tent.

"Where are you going?" I asked.

He pointed to the cluster of trees grouped at the corners of the high-peaked structure. "To knock on wood of course."

CHAPTER 3

"Get back here," I said, reaching out and taking hold of Richard's sleeve. "No one is going to be murdered."

"The day is young, Annabelle," Richard said, glancing at Sidney Allen primping his masked performers on the dance floor.

"First things first." I twisted to face Kate. "You and the bride get along well, right?"

"She does follow me on Instagram and comments on almost all my posts. In social media terms, that means we're practically best friends."

"Perfect. Can you go have a chat with the bride while I check the reception setup?" I pulled my phone out of my pocket and held it up. "Text me if you need reinforcements."

Kate gave me a thumbs up and headed inside.

I glanced at Fern who remained next to me. "Don't you need to get back to the bridal party?"

"Those tramps are fine." Fern waved a hand at me. "But when I say tramps, this time I mean it."

"You call all your clients tramps," I reminded him. It used to fluster me that Fern referred to all his high-society hair clients by raunchy names until I realized he used the same words on everyone, and the clients seemed to find it funny.

"Or hussies," Richard added. "Or trollops."

Fern beamed at Richard. "Thanks for reminding me about that one. I haven't called someone a trollop in ages. It's such a classic word too."

"I take it this isn't your easiest bridal party?" I asked.

Fern gave me a look that told me this was an understatement. "These girls take catty to the next level. The college friends don't like the high school friends, and those girls don't like the work friend. Then there's a girl from the wrong side of who knows where."

I'd seen this before. Mixing women from different phases of life didn't always lead to harmony and lifelong bonds.

Richard swept an arm wide. "We're in Potomac. There isn't a railroad track to be on the wrong side of out here. Everyone's absurdly wealthy."

Fern arched a brow. "You'll see. I promise you these are not your usual rich girls gone slightly wild."

"What about the bride's younger sister?" I asked, remembering the brunette from a few of our meetings. "She seems okay."

"She's fine, if not a little resentful. She doesn't have the personality of her sister though."

Fern was right there. The bride was larger than life. Not what I'd call beautiful in a traditional sense, but Veronica was tall and voluptuous with an infectious laugh and the talent to draw people to her. She was also dramatic and prone to what could generously be called tantrums, which is why I wasn't overly concerned about her latest stunt.

"Should I send up more champagne?" Richard asked. "Better yet, should I send up more food?"

Fern gave an abrupt shake of his head. "No more booze for these tramps, and don't send one of your cute waiters again. The last one almost got mauled, poor thing. Don't you have any middle-aged waiters with a dad bod?"

"Bite your tongue," Richard said. "Haven't we already established that I like my staff to be as visually appealing as my food?"

I studied Fern. "You look remarkably sober today, come to think of it."

"I have to keep my wits about me." He gestured to a man in black pants and a black blazer pacing the perimeter of the open-sided dinner tent and then disappearing around the back of the draped cocktail hour tent behind it. "There are men with guns here. Lots of them."

"That's the dad's private security," I said. "Unless you try to attack him, you should be fine."

We all looked over as Sidney Allen screeched something about his performers riding around in golf carts and took off waddling across the lawn. For the tenth time that day, I felt lucky not to work for him, and I didn't blame his employees for trying to escape in a golf cart, although I'd have to remind the staff that the carts the family used to visit their stables were not to be used for joyriding.

"There are worse things than being shot," Richard said, eyeing the hysterical entertainment diva as the man screeched orders into his headset.

"With that in mind, I'd better head back to the lion's den." Fern fluffed the red scarf tied at his neck and headed inside. "I hope Kate's been able to coax Veronica out of the bathroom. It will be much harder to do her beachy waves through a door."

Richard's phone trilled from inside his jacket and he pulled it out, giving an impatient huff when he looked at the screen and answered. "Leatrice, darling. You know I'm grateful to you for watching Hermes, but you do remember I'm working a wedding, right?"

He rolled his eyes and shook his head, pointing to the phone as he listened. My slightly eccentric neighbor, Leatrice, loved only one thing more than meddling in my personal life, and that was taking care of Richard's tiny Yorkie, Hermes. Although Richard had declared himself firmly in the 'no pets and children' camp for as long as I'd known him, the miniature pup had come part and parcel with his current significant other. Despite his protests, Richard had taken to the little dog and toted him around in his man bag, giving new meaning to the phrase "purse dog." When he and his partner were both working, Leatrice reveled in her time with Hermes.

"What do you mean 'does he get scared easily'?" Richard asked into the phone. "Of course it's fine for him to watch an R-rated movie. He's a dog."

I put a hand to my mouth to keep from laughing.

"But no popcorn or candy. It's bad for him, and you know he only eats organic." Richard tapped his foot on the paving stones. "Fine, but keep him on the leash. He gets overly excited when he sees the elephants."

I waited for him to hang up. "It sounds like Leatrice and Hermes are having a better day than we are."

Richard flicked a hand through his unmoving hair. "First they're having a Hitchcock marathon, and then they may go to the zoo."

"That's normal." Of course it was all relative considering the fact that Hermes had a considerable wardrobe of designer outfits—including a Burberry raincoat that matched Richard's—and both dog and owner were on the Paleo diet.

My phone vibrated, and I looked at the name popping up on the screen. Detective Reese. My stomach fluttered, and I angled the phone so Richard couldn't see.

"Did Kate have success already?" he asked, watching me fumble with my phone.

"No, it's nothing important." I dropped the phone in my pocket. "Nothing wedding related at least."

Richard looked away. "You'd think a detective would be able to figure out it's not a good idea to call a wedding planner in the middle of a wedding day."

I didn't respond as I made my way across the pool deck and into the dinner tent, stepping onto the wooden flooring we'd installed so women wouldn't spend the entire night with their heels sinking into the grass. Round tables draped in shimmering silver cloths filled most of the tent, with a shiny white dance floor in the center of the space. A glittering crystal chandelier hung over the dance floor, and smaller versions hung throughout the rest of the tent. Silver candelabra on each table were surrounded by masses of white flowers and jeweled Venetian masks. At each place setting, an ornate mask lay across the silver base plate, the guest's name on a tag tied on with iridescent ribbon.

"You know, Annabelle," Richard followed me, "you don't have to pretend he isn't calling. It's not like I'm oblivious to your relationship."

"Are you kidding me?" I slipped off my black flats before stepping onto the dance floor. "You either ignore him or glare at him every time the two of you are in the same room."

Richard inhaled sharply. "That's absurd."

"Agreed." I stared at him. "So what are we going to do about this?"

He pressed a palm to his chest. "Are you implying I'm the problem here?"

I adjusted the name tag on a mask that was adorned with silver feathers. "You've had an issue with Reese since the second he showed interest in me. And since we've been dating, you've been almost hostile to him. What's going to happen if we move in together?"

Richard staggered back a few steps. "Move in together? Are you serious?"

"I don't know." I really didn't know if I was ready to move in with my boyfriend, and now I regretted mentioning it to Richard. "It's a possibility."

"Has this been discussed?" Richard's voice dropped so low I could barely hear him over the sounds of the band setting up on the stage behind us.

"Kind of." Reese had mentioned it once, but we hadn't discussed it any further. My stammered response to him might have had something to do with that. "Nothing's been settled, but it's on the table."

"And this is the first I'm hearing about this major life decision?" Richard sniffed. "Well, it looks like you don't need my input anymore."

"Come on," I said, moving to another table and repositioning a gilded mask with a multicolored Harlequin pattern. "Why does this have to be a big deal?"

"Because moving in with someone is a big deal. It's one step closer to you running off and getting married." His voice cracked. "And that will change everything."

I noticed a few stares from the band's sound crew as they moved the speakers into place. "I have no plans to run off and get married."

"You say that now, but fast forward a year and you're walking down the aisle toward tall, dark, and testosterone. And where am I in all this?" He dabbed at his eyes. "I'll tell you where. Nowhere. Pushed out. There can't be two main men in your life, and I'll be the one kicked to the curb."

"That will never happen."

Richard took a long breath. "We already spend less time together. When is the last time I came over to cook because you had nothing in the house and can barely boil water?"

I tried to remember the last night Richard and I had spent hanging out at my place together. I hated to admit I couldn't.

He pulled away from me. "Face it, darling. It's already happened."

I opened and closed my mouth as he stalked off out of the tent, the band members making a point of looking away. I wanted to call him back, but I didn't know what to say. I also didn't want to make any more of a scene in front of other wedding vendors than we already had.

Maybe he was right and I was moving too fast with Reese. I did know the thought of moving in with him—or anyone—made my stomach do flips, and I wasn't sure if they were the good kind of flips. I'd been living on my own for so long that the idea of giving up any bit of independence made me nervous. I liked coming and going on my own schedule and not answering to anyone but my nosy neighbor. Would I be giving that up by moving in with Reese?

The thought of losing my friends was even worse. Richard had been my mentor and support system since I moved to DC seven years ago and started my own wedding planning business. He'd stuck with me when I'd sent him clients who insisted on putting garden gnomes on the buffet, and when I'd inadvertently gotten him mixed up in multiple murder investigations. Losing him would be like cutting off one of my arms.

I felt my phone buzz and gave an impatient groan. If Reese was going to call me all day, it was not going to help his case. I pulled out my phone and looked at the screen. It was a text from Kate but only a series of random letters. Either she butt dialed me or was having a stroke. I typed back 'What?' and pressed send.

I didn't get a response, so I slipped my phone back into my pocket. She must already have her phone on mute. I decided I'd better go upstairs and check on the bride myself. I gave a final, envious glance at the swimming penguins as I crossed back through the pool deck and opened the French doors leading into the house. The noise of splashing penguins and band sound checks were replaced with an Andrea Bocelli song, and I remembered the opera singer whom I'd told could practice in the library. I'd barely made it two steps into the kitchen when Fern rushed into the room.

"Thank heavens I found you." He stopped to catch his breath when he reached me.

"What's wrong?" I asked, grabbing him by the shoulders.

"It's . . . the bride." His words came out in stops and starts. "She's gone."

CHAPTER 4

"*M*issing?" I asked Fern as I stood in the bride's upstairs bedroom. "How can she be missing?"

The bridesmaids were down the hall in the sister's bedroom with the makeup artist, so the sunny room stood empty and silent. A king size sleigh bed was covered in a white duvet piped in pale blue and stacked with a variety of white-and-blue pillows, as well as several stuffed penguins. A tall wooden wardrobe was positioned across from the bed with the wedding dress hanging from one of the open doors, the full organza skirt billowing to the floor. The matching vanity by the window was covered with hairdryers, bottles of styling serum, and bobby pins, the tufted stool pulled out at an angle as if the bride had just gotten up. Sheer curtains covered the wide window that overlooked the pool, the rolling hills behind the house, and the stables in the distance.

I crossed to the mahogany vanity where a half-full flute of champagne with lipstick marks on the rim sat next to a natural bristle brush. The scent of hairspray and perfume lingered in the air.

"When I came up to see how much progress Kate was making with Veronica, this is what I found." Fern indicated the door to the en suite bathroom hanging open. "I assumed she was getting makeup done down the hall and went to check there, but no luck."

I leaned into the bathroom. Nothing but a lot of beige tile carved with scrolls and flowers, a garden tub surrounded by jars of bath salts, a glass-doored shower, and a long stretch of marble with two sinks and a sizable collection of Crème de la Mer products. A quick check of the door in the corner revealed the toilet and a bidet, not that I expected to find the bride hiding in there.

I went back to the bedroom and sat on the tufted bench at the end of the bed. I could hear the giggles and chatter from the bridal party from a few doors away. I rubbed my temples. "She can't really have run off," I said, trying to convince myself more than anyone. "That's so dramatic, even for her."

Fern joined me on the bench, crossing his legs at the knee. "I checked all the rooms upstairs and did a quick run through of the main rooms downstairs before I came to get you. I thought there was an outside chance she might have gone to the kitchen for a bite."

I shook my head. "She would have sent Kate if she needed something. Which reminds me, where is Kate?"

"I thought she was with you, and I'd missed her somehow when I came upstairs and ran around looking for the bride."

I sat up straighter. "This is good news. If Kate is with Veronica, they can't be far. Kate would never let her do a 'runaway bride.'" I pulled out my phone and texted her. "They must be somewhere in the house."

Fern's shoulders relaxed. "Of course you're right. It's a huge house after all. Maybe Veronica wanted to get away from the bridesmaids and convinced Kate to go with her."

"Did you know there are twelve bathrooms in this place?" I asked Fern as I stared at the screen of my phone waiting for a reply to my text.

"Goodness." Fern wrinkled his nose. "Can you imagine having to clean all of those?"

"No, and I don't want to have to search all of them or the twenty or so other rooms in this place."

A long, white box appeared in the doorway, seeming to hover in midair until a man's bald head joined it, followed by the rest of his body. "Is this where the bouquets should go?"

"You're in the right place," I told Mack, one half of the flower designing duo also known as the Mighty Morphin Flower Arrangers.

Mack set the box on the bed and stepped back, putting his hands on the waist of his black leather pants.

"No vest today?" Fern asked, appraising the man's outfit of white T-shirt, leather pants, and black motorcycle boots.

Usually the outfit included leather vests complete with chains, which made it easy to hear them coming. Today, without their vests, they were in stealth mode.

"Too hot," Mack's partner, Buster, said as he came into the room carrying a smaller white box I guessed was the boutonnieres.

Buster and Mack were the owners of Lush, one of DC's top floral designers for weddings. They were known for dramatic designs and for their notable appearance. Both men topped six feet tall and three hundred pounds, were bald with goatees, and wore lots of black leather. Even though they were similar, Mack's hair—what little he had—was dark red while Buster's goatee was brown, and Buster always wore a pair of motorcycle goggles on top of his head.

Fern swung his crossed leg. "I'm lucky I don't perspire."

"You're lucky you don't know what it's like to sweat in leather pants," Buster said.

I knew it would be foolish to suggest they wear shorts or breathable fabrics since they rode Harleys even when coming to weddings.

Mack did a quick scan of the room. "Where's the bride? We want to show her the bouquets and make sure she likes them."

I exchanged a look with Fern. "The bride is . . . not here."

Mack raised his pierced eyebrow. "Where is she?"

Fern cupped a hand around one side of his mouth and said in a stage whisper, "We don't know."

Buster gave me a questioning look. "Is this true? We don't know where the bride is?"

"Technically only one-half of the Wedding Belles team is in the dark on the bride's location," I said. "Kate is with her somewhere, and I'm sure she'll text me any moment to tell me where."

We all looked at my phone, which did not vibrate or ring.

Fern rested a hand on my knee. "We should face facts, sweetie. The bride has done a runner, and Kate is her accomplice."

Mack's mouth fell open a bit. "Cheese and crackers! We've never had a groom left at the altar before."

"I could go for some cheese and crackers right about now," Fern said, touching a hand to his flat stomach.

As members of a Christian biker gang, Buster and Mack made it a rule not to swear, which led to some interesting expressions during times of stress.

"This groom will not be left at the altar," I assured Mack, although I didn't feel so confident. Where was Kate, and why wasn't she answering my texts?

I stood up as my phone rang, swiping to talk without checking who was calling. "Kate, where are you?"

"Not Kate," Richard said, "but where are *you*?"

"In the bride's room." I lowered my voice. "We can't find her or Kate."

Richard was silent for a moment, and I thought I'd lost the call. "What do you mean you can't find them?"

"When Fern came to the room, it was empty. He did a quick search of the rooms and had no luck. I've texted Kate but haven't heard back."

Richard's breath became more ragged. "Do you think the bride ran off before the wedding? Tell me now, Annabelle, before my chefs start caramelizing the Brie tartlets."

"Kate would never aid and abet a bride in running out on her own wedding. She knows I'd kill her."

"You'd have to get in line," Richard muttered.

"I'm going to have a look around the house. They have to be here somewhere."

"And I'm helping her," Fern said, leaning over toward the phone.

"We will too," Buster added in his deep rumble of a voice.

"Well, that's comforting," Richard said. "We have a gondolier and two Christian bikers on the case."

I tapped my foot against the plush carpet. "If you want to help, you could look yourself. We have a lot of rooms to get through."

"Fine. I'll take the pool house," Richard said. "It's the closest room to our makeshift kitchen setup in the garage."

"Call me the second you find them," I said before clicking off.

"Buster and I will take the basement level," Mack said. "Maybe they're downstairs in the movie theatre."

"You don't think they're watching *The Notebook*, do you?" Fern asked, jumping to his feet. "Kate and I adore that movie. Maybe I should go with you two to check."

I pulled Fern to my side as he tried to leave with the florists. "You're with me, and we have no time for matinees. We'll take the main level since you already searched all the bedrooms."

Fern made a pouty face but followed me out of the bedroom behind Buster and Mack and down the sweeping staircase to the foyer. The two burly men continued downstairs while Fern and I walked through the living room with its soaring cathedral ceiling and massive fireplace. A slim man in a tuxedo paced at the far end, humming scales. He paused when he saw us.

"Don't mind us," I told the man I recognized as our opera singer.

We popped our heads into the father's empty study as I heard the tenor begin to sing again. We passed several waiters in long white bistro aprons over their black pants when we entered the open kitchen and informal dining room that stretched across the back of the house. I glanced out the glass walls facing the pool. There was plenty of activity under the dinner tent as the band set up and the final touches were put on the décor by the floral staff, but I didn't see Kate or the bride. There was no one in the formal dining room with the oval table that could seat twenty or in the den with the sectional sofa and big-screen TV mounted over another fireplace.

Fern threw up his hands. "That's it."

"You're forgetting the rooms off the garage." I motioned for him to follow me.

"Why would they be hiding out in the mud room or the assistant's office?" Fern asked as I opened the door to the office of the mother of the bride's personal assistant. The lights were off, and no one sat behind the wooden desk.

"We have to check everything." I pulled the door closed and stepped into the mud room with its shelving unit and series of cubbies.

Fern motioned to the baskets tucked in the tall white unit. "Not in here unless they used a shrink ray."

We retraced our steps to the kitchen, and I stopped short when I spotted a woman with tightly curled gray hair, wearing a floral bathrobe, rifling through the kitchen drawers.

"Can I help you?" I asked.

The woman looked up. "You can if you've got any ciggies."

"Ciggies?" Fern snapped his fingers as a look of recognition passed across his face. "Oh, you mean cigarettes."

"Yeah, cigarettes." The woman looked at us like we were slow. "You got any?"

Fern and I exchanged a look.

"No we don't," I said. "Do you mind me asking who you are?"

The woman sighed and closed a dark wood drawer, turning her attention to the overhead cabinets. "I'm the granny, I mean grand-mother." She cleared her throat and it sounded like she was hacking up a hairball. "The bride's grandmother."

From creating the ceremony program, I knew Veronica only had one living grandmother, and it was her mother's mother. I looked at this woman with her raspy voice and her frizzy perm and tried to see the connection with the sophisticated Mrs. Hamilton.

"I know my daughter keeps cigarettes hidden somewhere." She put her hands on her hips. "If I could only find them."

I'd never seen the mother of the bride smoke, and I wondered if this was a habit she'd kicked long ago.

"Sorry," I said. "I can't help you there."

"You haven't seen your granddaughter recently, have you?" Fern asked.

The woman moved the chrome espresso machine and peered behind it. "Which one?"

"The bride," I said. "Veronica."

She gave a half laugh, half snort. "The princess didn't want family around her while she got ready, so I haven't seen her all day." She shrugged. "Fine by me."

Fern raised his eyebrows.

The old woman's head snapped up. "You don't think she has smokes in her room do you?"

"The bride doesn't smoke," I said.

The grandmother cackled as she lifted the lids off two white ceramic containers sitting to one side of the shiny black stovetop and looked inside. "Sure she doesn't."

Was this woman crazy? I'd had plenty of clients who smoked, but Veronica and her mother had never once smelled like smoke, and I'd never seen packs of cigarettes in their purses or anywhere in the house. You might be able to disguise a drinking habit with mints and mouthwash, but smoke lingered in your hair and clothes and was a dead giveaway.

The woman slammed the drawer shut and made for the doorway leading to the foyer. "Guess I'll keep looking upstairs." She leveled a finger at us as she passed. "Don't tell my daughter you saw me. I'm not in the mood for a lecture."

"Well, she's a piece of work," Fern said, staring at the doorway the woman had exited. "No wonder they've kept her hidden away until now."

Mack barreled through the doorway with Buster fast on his heels and almost knocked into us.

He grasped my shoulders to stop himself and keep me from falling over. "Thank the good Lord we found you."

"What's up?" I asked, noticing the worried expression on his face.

"We found this outside the front door." Mack held up a phone.

I took the iPhone from him and flipped it over, recognizing Kate's custom cover with the Wedding Belles logo. My pulse quickened. "This is Kate's phone."

Buster nodded. "She must have dropped it."

"That explains why she wasn't responding to you." Fern patted my hand. "At least you know she wasn't ignoring you. That should make you feel better."

"And it was outside by the front door?" I asked.

Buster pressed his lips together without answering.

"Maybe the bride did run off and Kate went with her," I said, even though I couldn't believe Kate would do such a thing. "Or maybe they ran out for something, and Kate dropped her phone so she can't tell us where they are."

"I'm sure that's it," Mack said, a look of relief crossing his face. "Maybe it was a supply run."

Fern snapped his fingers. "Or the bride was in the mood for fries. Do you remember the bride who made us take the limo through the McDonald's drive-thru for fries?"

I let out a breath, but my heart did not slow. "That's true. Brides can be insistent, especially this one. If she'd wanted to leave the house for some reason, I doubt Kate could have stopped her."

Mack put an arm around my shoulder as he led me toward the kitchen table. "I'm sure this is a big to-do over nothing."

A scream pierced the air and we all jumped.

"Who was that?" Fern asked, staggering against the marble countertop.

I half expected Richard to come running in from the makeshift kitchen in the garage, screaming bloody murder about his chef ruining the hollandaise sauce. When I looked up to see the mother of the bride staggering into the room from the far end, it took me a second to realize she'd been the one to scream. She wore a black silk bathrobe that reached the floor and had her brown hair in curlers. Her eyes were wide, and her hands shook as she leaned against one of the dining chairs.

Fern rushed to her before she collapsed onto the floor. "Are you hurt?"

She shook her head as she slumped against Fern. "It's Veronica. They've kidnapped my daughter."

Kate's phone slipped out of my hand and clattered to the floor.

CHAPTER 5

"*B*reathe deeply," I said, rubbing Fern's back as he bent over double with his hands on his knees.

Fern fanned his face. "It's just such a shock."

I turned to the bride's mother, who sat at the oval kitchen table between Buster and Mack. "Can I get you anything, Mrs. Hamilton?"

She motioned to the glass of ice water sitting in front of her. "I'm fine. I should be getting back to my husband though. He's the one who got the ransom call."

I took a seat across the table, forcing myself to remain calm, even though my hands were shaking and I felt like I might throw up. "Can you run through what happened again? It was hard to hear with all the shrieking going on earlier."

"Excuse me for being startled by the news," Fern muttered from his upside-down position.

A waiter came inside through one of the French doors, and I could hear the sounds of the band tuning on the stage. I looked outside and saw the penguin handler drying off her charges with fluffy yellow towels I recognized from the pool house. My eyes went to the far end of the pool and the building that looked like a minia-ture Italian villa. I remembered Richard had been headed there to look for Kate and the bride, but I didn't see him. I hoped he was busy in the garage kitchen and oblivious to the kidnapping. I had enough on my plate with Fern. The last thing I needed was a Richard meltdown.

"Of course." Mrs. Hamilton took a sip of water, the ice cubes clinking in the glass. "My husband was in our bedroom getting dressed when his cell phone rang. I started to get upset with him for answering it on our daughter's wedding day—he's always taking calls from his business partner—but as soon as I saw his face, I knew it wasn't that."

Mack reached over and squeezed her hand.

"Did your husband recognize the number?" I asked.

"I don't know. He didn't say." She pressed a hand to her pale cheek. "I do know he didn't recognize the voice on the other end, because it was disguised by one of those voice changers. I could hear it a little, and it sounded warped."

I'd heard voice changing software on TV shows, so I knew what she meant.

"The voice said they had Veronica, and if we wanted to see her again alive, he would pay the ransom." Mrs. Hamilton began weeping quietly as Buster put an arm around her shoulder.

"Did they mention Kate?" I asked.

The bride's mother looked up at me with a blank look on her face. "Who?"

"My assistant, Kate. She was with Veronica earlier, and we found her phone on the floor near the front door. She's also missing, and I think she may have been taken because she was with your daughter."

"No, they didn't," Mrs. Hamilton said. "I'm sorry."

I was sorry too. If Kate had been taken because she was in the way, I couldn't help but worry that she'd be easily discarded. What if they thought there was no reason to keep her, or if it was a hassle to have two hostages?

"I'm sure she's fine," Mack said, his pinched face not conveying the same confidence as his words. "Kate's a tough one."

Fern gave a strangled sob.

"Have you contacted the police?" I asked.

Mrs. Hamilton jerked her head back and forth. "The kidnappers said no law enforcement. If they see any police, they'll kill her." She glanced out the windows. "They said they were watching us."

I couldn't imagine how since the estate wasn't within visual distance of the nearest neighbor, but I also wouldn't have thought anyone would have been able to kidnap two women out from under our noses.

"What about your husband's security team?"

Her face darkened. "You mean the team he hired to protect himself? They're so focused on watching for any threats against him, they weren't paying any attention to the rest of us."

I imagined this was an issue she'd be discussing at length with her husband. "So they didn't see anything?"

"Not that I know of." She pulled her silky robe closed tighter around her throat. "My husband is having them lock down the house and question everyone here, but it's too little too late if you ask me. At the moment, all I care about is paying the ransom and getting my daughter back safe."

I wanted to add "and Kate," but I didn't think the bride's mother remembered or cared that my assistant had been swept up into the situation. "We still have the wedding cake being delivered. Should I cancel it in light of the circumstances?"

Mrs. Hamilton put her hands to her cheeks. "The wedding cake. I forgot about that. I'll have my husband tell the security guards to let the baker in."

"So we should still go ahead with the wedding setup?" I asked. "I have a few more vendors who should be arriving later. Maybe I should tell them not to come."

Mrs. Hamilton stood, her curlers bobbing around her head and her jaw set. "No. The best thing we can do right now is assume that Veronica will be back in time to walk down the aisle. Give a list of your vendors to the security team, and I'll tell my husband to make sure they're let in."

"Not postpone?" Buster asked.

The bride's mother squared her shoulders. "We are getting Veronica back today, and she is getting married. I can't consider any other option."

I watched the woman swish out of the room and wished I felt as confident as she did. Even if they got Veronica back, would Kate be part of the deal?

"What about Kate?" Mack asked, voicing my thoughts. "I'm sure she's with the bride."

I bit the edge of my lower lip. My stomach churned at the thought of my assistant, who'd become one of my closest friends over the years we'd worked together, being held hostage somewhere. I stood up. "I need to make a call."

I ducked out of the kitchen and into the hallway that led to the garage. The door at the end opened, and I saw Sidney Allen's head bobbing behind a pair of minstrels in purple-and-green-satin costumes, holding lutes.

"Your songs don't sound Venetian enough," he said, his Southern accent drawing the word Venetian out an extra few syllables. "This is Carnival, people. Not cocktail hour at the Goldman bar mitzvah." He clapped his hands. "I need more energy."

The two minstrels rolled their eyes.

The last person I wanted to see was Sidney Allen and his not-so-merry band of performers. I opened the nearest door and slipped into the small windowless office of Mrs. Hamilton's personal assistant. I'd been in this room a couple of times during the planning process to drop off documents to be signed. As I pressed the speed dial on my phone, I closed the door behind me to block out the sound of Sidney Allen. Hearing a lecture on how to sound authentically Venetian delivered with a Southern twang was something I could go a lifetime without hearing. I perched on the edge of the messy desk and counted the rings, saying a small prayer that he would pick up.

"Hey, babe. How's the wedding going?" Detective Mike Reese asked when he answered.

Tears of relief sprang to my eyes when I heard his voice. "Not great." I heard my voice crack and took a breath to steady it.

33

"What's wrong?" His voice changed from playful to concerned.

"Kate's been kidnapped, along with the bride." As hard as I tried to even my voice, I could hear the waver in it.

There was a long pause. "I'm on my way."

"You can't," I said. "The father of the bride got a ransom call and was told if he goes to the police, they'll kill the hostages."

"I won't come in a squad car. It will be me alone. I'm off duty and at home anyway." His voice softened. "Listen, babe. You're in over your head. I want to help."

I hesitated. "I don't know. If the parents found out I brought a cop in when they were told no cops, it would not be good."

"The parents are probably focused on getting their daughter back, right?" Reese didn't wait for me to answer. "Who's looking out for Kate in all this?"

"The mom didn't seem concerned that Kate is also missing." I choked back tears. "I'm scared something's going to happen to her if the kidnappers decide she's not valuable."

"I'm not going to let that happen." His voice became lighter. "If something happens to your assistant, who's to say you won't try to recruit me to work weddings with you? I have a vested interest in making sure we get Kate back as soon as possible."

I laughed. "Fair enough. But you can't tell anyone here you're a cop. Is there any way you can come in disguise?"

"Dressed as what?"

Another call beeped in, and I looked at the screen. "Hold on two seconds." I clicked over.

"I'm about to leave my studio," Alexandra, my go-to cake baker, said on the other end. "Did the bride decide yay or nay on the silver cake pedestal?"

"Yes, I mean yay," I said. "Can I ask you a huge favor?"

"You want me to bring extra sugar petals for you to snack on?" she asked with a giggle, knowing how much I relied on the gum paste rose petals she scattered around her cakes to give me a boost of energy late at night.

"Can you pick up a passenger on the way?"

"A passenger?"

"I know it sounds odd, but I'll explain everything when you get here," I said. When she agreed, I added, "And in case you get tempted to hit on him, he's taken."

"The plot thickens," Alexandra said. "Now I can't wait to see this guy."

I hung up after I'd given her Reese's address, and I switched back to the other line. "My cake baker is going to pick you up in a delivery van in five minutes."

"I'm riding in a cake delivery van?"

"Admit it," I said. "It's a great cover. You'll be able to drive up to the house without anyone questioning you."

"I have to say, dating you is never boring."

"Mike," I said, closing my eyes and leaning back against the desk, "thank you for coming."

"Don't mention it, babe."

I clicked off and put my phone back in my pocket, feeling a sense of calm. Even if Reese wasn't officially on duty, he would know how to handle things.

I stood up to go back to the kitchen when the office door opened, and the mother of the bride's personal assistant stepped inside. I'd met the middle-aged blonde—Sherry, if I remembered correctly—a few times before, and she'd always seemed nice, if a bit harried. She paused when she saw me.

"I'm sorry. I needed a place where I could make a private phone call." I jerked a thumb in the direction of the kitchen. "It's a little dramatic out there."

The woman ran a hand through her short, wavy hair and grinned. "Tell me about it. I was coming in here to escape the chaos myself."

"How's Mrs. Hamilton handling everything?" I asked. I felt safe in assuming Sherry knew about the kidnapping since she was the mother's right-hand woman.

"Not great. She and Mr. Hamilton are having it out upstairs." Sherry sidestepped to the other side of her desk and pulled a bottle of Jameson's Irish Whiskey and a stack of Dixie paper cups from a drawer, pushing a pile of papers out of the way as she set both on the top of her desk. "Another reason I came down here."

"Why is she mad at her husband?"

Sherry twisted the cap off the bottle and poured a shot into each mini cup, holding one out to me. "I can be honest with you, right? We're both in the position of keeping our boss's secrets."

"Absolutely," I said, taking the cup from her so as not to be rude.

"The Hamiltons aren't the happiest couple on the block. Never have been, and I've been with them from pretty much the beginning. Mrs. Hamilton likes the money, but not the strings that come with it. And now this." Sherry's voice was deep and throaty, and I wondered if she ever paired cigarettes with her whiskey. "She blames him for her daughter being taken."

I held the whiskey without drinking it. "Just because he's wealthy?"

Sherry slammed back her whiskey and motioned for me to do the same. "He was already wealthy before he got involved with DOD. Mrs. Hamilton thinks the new defense contracts are why someone targeted Veronica. It's why he had to hire bodyguards."

I took a sip of my whiskey and tried not to gasp as it seared my throat. "But why would his work with the Department of Defense increase the chances his daughter would be kidnapped? Because they can ask for a bigger ransom?"

Sherry eyed the whiskey bottle and poured herself another. "You don't know?"

"Know what?" I took another tiny drink, noticing the way it warmed my stomach and loosened the knot between my shoulders.

"The kidnappers aren't asking for money." Sherry lowered her voice even though the door was closed. "They want Mr. Hamilton to bring them some of the nerve gas he's been developing."

I set the paper cup back on the desk before my shaking hands spilled it. "So these aren't your run-of-the-mill kidnappers? They're terrorists?"

CHAPTER 6

"What do you mean they don't want money?" Fern asked me after I'd pulled him, Buster, and Mack outside to the pool deck to tell them what I'd learned. I didn't need to keep my voice low since the band's sound checks meant I could scream the news and still not be the loudest noise outside.

A steady stream of waiters flowed back and forth from the garage kitchen to the dinner tent carrying baskets of bread sticks and silver pitchers of water, but I did not see Richard. I wondered if he was inside the smaller fabric-draped cocktail tent, but since there was little setup to do in the space, I doubted it. I felt relieved. I didn't look forward to breaking the news to him that no one would get to see his mask-shaped breadsticks.

"This ransom is about getting access to the nerve agent the dad's company has been developing for the DOD." I held up a hand to shield my eyes from the sun and stepped under a patio umbrella for shade. "They want poison gas instead of cash."

Fern gasped and leaned against one of the patio tables, causing the tan-and-white-striped umbrella over us to wobble. "It's like we're in a James Bond movie." He glanced at the two penguins lounging on chairs by the pool. "Or a Disney movie gone wrong."

LAURA DURHAM

"This is awful," Buster said. "I can't imagine something worse happening at a wedding."

I had to agree with him, and considering some of the disasters we'd had, that was saying something.

Mack lowered himself into one of the patio chairs with a thud. "So Kate and the bride were taken by a group of terrorists?"

"According to Mrs. Hamilton's personal assistant," I said. "And I tend to believe her since she's been the one to give me the inside track since we started planning."

Buster put a hand on Mack's shoulder. "We should activate the prayer chain."

As part of the Road Riders for Jesus motorcycle gang, they had a prayer chain they credited with finding me a boyfriend, saving Twinkies from being discontinued, and averting a hurricane.

I shook my head. "We have to keep this between us. If this gets out, it could put Kate and Veronica in danger."

Mack reached up and patted Buster's hand. "Two can pray just as hard."

I felt tears prick the back of my eyes as I thought of Kate being held hostage and the real danger she was in. I pushed the images out of my head and cleared my throat. "Detective Reese is on his way with Alexandra, but no one but us can know he's a cop."

"Who is he supposed to be?" Fern asked, dabbing his eyes with a linen handkerchief monogrammed with a swirling F.

"For now he's a cake delivery guy," I said. "I know the kidnappers said no cops, but we need someone who knows what they're doing and who can help us save Kate. I'm afraid the Hamiltons aren't focused on anything but getting Veronica back."

"Do *not* tell me the bride is still MIA."

I hadn't heard Richard come up behind us over all the noise from the band, and it was clear he'd only heard the tail end of our conversation. His hand rested on one jutted-out hip, and he tilted his head at me.

"You might need to sit down for this," I told him, indicating the cushioned chair next to Mack.

His eyes searched our faces. "What's going on? Is the wedding canceled? I hope the parents know that I'm going to bill them whether their daughter walks down the aisle or not."

"The bride didn't run off," Fern said, blowing his nose loudly into his handkerchief.

"Thank heavens," Richard said, releasing a breath before narrowing his eyes at me. "Then why the grim faces? Is it the groom? Did he finally realize what a brat the bride is? I could understand if he ran off. I always thought that boy was in way over his head."

"No one ran off," I said. "The bride was kidnapped."

Richard blinked at me. "I beg your pardon?"

"And they took Kate too," Mack added, putting his head in his thick hands.

Richard staggered into a patio chair. "Kidnapped? I don't understand. When did this happen?"

"Sometime between when Kate went upstairs to talk to the bride and when Fern went back up to check on them," I said. "The father of the bride got a call from the kidnappers a few minutes ago."

"And Kate?" Richard asked, looking up at me.

I steadied my voice before answering. "With Veronica we think. Her phone was on the floor by the front door."

"How could this happen?" Buster shifted his weight, and his leather pants creaked. "How do you drag off a bride and a wedding planner in the middle of wedding setup? There are people everywhere."

"That's exactly how," I said, feeling a bead of sweat trickle down my back even though I stood in the shade. "There are so many people, we'd never notice a few extra. Not to mention the trucks and vans that have been coming and going all day."

Mack pointed to a pair of men clad in black emerging from around the side of the house, the gun bulges obvious underneath their blazers. One of the men spoke into his wrist, and the pair strode toward the tent. "It looks like the security guards are springing into action."

"I'll bet they're in hot water for having someone kidnapped under their watch," I said, watching the men begin to question the band. "Although I think they were specifically hired to watch the dad." I pulled my schedule out of my pocket and ripped off one of the pages I'd already used. I leaned over a nearby table and began writing. "I need to give them a list of vendors who still need to get on the property."

"Will there be a list of people who get to leave as well?" Buster asked.

I looked up from making my list. "You want to take off?"

Mack shot his partner a look. "We would never in a million years think of abandoning you at a time like this."

"I don't want to leave," Buster said, "but we do have another wedding downtown."

Mack dismissed Buster's concerns with a shake of his head. "Our other setup crew can handle it. It's a tiny affair. Not to mention they slashed the floral budget until it's practically miniscule. You can't expect to get the Mighty Morphin Flower Arrangers in person when you only order bud vases." Another head shake. "We're staying with you."

I felt a bit bad for the people who'd had the temerity to order single flower arrangements from Lush, but not bad enough to surrender Buster and Mack. I felt like I needed all the emotional support I could get, not to mention as many eyes and ears as possible to find out what was really going on. I finished my list, making sure to include the band members who would arrive right before the performance, Alexandra and her phony delivery assistant Mike Reese, the female officiant, and the groomsmen who were getting ready at a nearby hotel and would arrive before the ceremony. If we had a ceremony.

"Be right back." I made my way over to the nearest member of the security team and dabbed at the sweat gathering on my upper lip. I knew these guys weren't actual cops, but their severe demeanor and gun bulges gave me pause.

One of the men looked up as I approached. "Can I help you?"

I steadied my voice and told myself I had no reason to feel flustered, especially since these guys were glorified rent-a-cops. "Mrs. Hamilton asked me to give you a list of people who should be allowed on the property."

He slid his mirrored sunglasses onto the top of his head and took the paper I held out. "And you are?"

I laughed but heard the quaver in it. "Annabelle Archer. The wedding planner."

The man folded the paper and slid it into his blazer pocket, exposing his holstered gun. "I'll take care of it."

His body language did not invite conversation, but I couldn't stop myself from trying. I jutted one hip out and gave him my most seductive smile. "Any idea how the kidnappers got the bride and my assistant away from the house?"

"Your assistant?" He studied me, his expression unchanging.

"Yes, my assistant, Kate." Did anyone else even care she was missing? "She was with Veronica, and they're both missing."

His eyebrow flickered slightly. "I didn't know that. But to answer your question, I can't."

I leaned forward on my toes, trying to flutter my eyelashes like Kate had taught me.

"Do you have something wrong with your eye?"

I stopped fluttering and could hear a muffled guffaw behind me. Richard, no doubt. "No, I'm fine. You can't what?"

"Can't answer your question," he said. "Mr. Hamilton has given us strict instructions not to contact law enforcement or talk to anyone about the situation."

I let out a breath. This did not surprise me, but it didn't make me happy, either. "Well, I happen to know just about every person who's on-site today for the wedding. When you realize you need my help, I'll be around." I spun on my heel a little too fast and had to put my arms out to keep myself from falling over. I cursed at myself silently for ruining my own dramatic exit as I walked back to my friends.

"I'm just sorry that Kate missed you trying to use your feminine wiles on that man," Richard said.

"Ignore him, sweetie." Fern put a hand around my waist. "Eyelash batting is an advanced technique. It takes skill to make it look like you're not having a seizure."

"Who knew Kate's skills were so useful?" I said.

Richard raised and lowered one shoulder. "Half the single men in the metropolitan area?"

Mack wagged a finger at him. "You shouldn't speak ill of the kidnapped."

"Au contraire," Richard said. "It's the dead I shouldn't speak ill of."

We fell silent, and Richard's tan lost a few shades. "You know I didn't mean . . ."

"We all know Kate is going to be fine," Buster said, his voice so forceful we all jumped. He balled his massive hands into fists. "And we're going to find whoever did this."

Mack gave a curt nod. "They have no idea who they've messed with."

I doubt the kidnappers had any clue they were up against a team of wedding professionals with an unusually high amount of crime-solving experience. Not to mention a couple of scary-looking bikers with a direct line to the Big Guy.

Fern looked over my head and his eyes lit up. "Is that who I think it is?"

CHAPTER 7

"Someone ordered a wedding cake?" Reese asked as he stepped out of the house carrying a wide cake box, followed by Alexandra pushing a wheeled trolley with more boxes stacked on its shelves.

Reese wore jeans and a white T-shirt with a black baseball hat covering his dark hair, looking every bit the delivery man. Alexandra wore a slim white pencil skirt and a pink chiffon blouse, with her long brown hair pulled up in a high ponytail, and looked nothing like any other baker I'd ever seen. I'd gotten used to the cake baker's glamour, but most people were surprised to learn the stunning woman created decadent wedding cakes for a living.

Richard's head snapped in my direction. "Please tell me I'm having a heat stroke and hallucinating."

"I thought he could help us get Kate back." I dropped my voice now that the band had stopped warming up. "No one can know he's a cop though. The kidnappers said no police, and the Hamiltons would not be happy if they knew I'd called in a detective."

"We're supposed to pretend he's a cake delivery man?" Fern asked, giving Reese the up and down as he sauntered toward us.

"The cake delivery ruse was to get him in, but it won't be believable when he's still here long after the cake has been set up." I tapped my finger against my chin. "We need another reason he would be here so he can stay and help us."

Reese held out the cake box when he reached me. "Wedding cake is heavier than I expected. Where should I put this?"

I took the white box and placed it on the patio table under the umbrella. "No trouble getting in?"

He motioned his head in Alexandra's direction. "She charmed the guard at the front gate."

Not surprising. If her looks didn't get them, the accent—a European lilt that Alexandra never narrowed down to more than "a bit of everywhere, darling"—usually did.

"There's a guard at the front gate?" I asked. "There wasn't one earlier."

"Security usually gets beefed up after a crime," Reese said. "Although this security looks like more than your standard rent-a-cop. I'd guess these guys are former military."

Alexandra stopped rolling the trolley when she reached us. "I can't set up a cake in this heat. It will melt before the bride makes it down the aisle."

"Richard has a special table on wheels for the cake," I said. "You can assemble it inside the kitchen, and we'll wheel it out right before cake cutting."

Alexandra gave me a slow wink I would have thought was suggestive if I didn't know her so well. "You think of everything."

Buster picked up the cake box on the table. "I'll take this inside for you." He moved his eyes between Reese and me. "That way you two can catch up."

Mack stood up and hurried after Alexandra and Buster as they disappeared into the house. "I'll help. The cake table needs lots of floral swag."

Reese put an arm around me. "How are you holding up?"

I allowed myself to lean into him. "I'm okay. Worried, but okay." I met his hazel eyes. "I'm glad you're here."

"We're going to get Kate back," he said, pulling me closer.

I nodded, but felt tears stinging my eyes so I looked down. We hadn't been going out long enough for him to see me ugly cry, which I might do if I thought about the situation for too long.

Richard cleared his throat. "So what's your plan, Detective?"

I put a finger to my lips. "He's not a detective, remember? This has to be on the down low."

"I could give him a disguise," Fern whispered. "Possibly hair extensions."

Reese's eyebrows disappeared beneath his hat.

"He doesn't need a disguise," I said, feeling Reese relax next to me. "A good cover will suffice."

"Let's worry about that later," Reese said. "First tell me what's being done to get the bride and Kate back."

"I don't know the details of the ransom call," I said. "But I do know the kidnappers didn't ask for money. They asked for some of the poison gas the dad's pharmaceutical company has been developing for the DOD."

Reese's eyes widened. "Are you serious?" He took off his hat and rubbed his forehead. "This isn't your run-of-the-mill kidnapping?"

"We're doomed." Richard slumped further down in his chair. "I should pack up my kitchen now. This wedding is never going to happen, and no one is ever going to see my spun sugar carnival masks."

I glared at him. "We're not doomed. We're going to get Kate and Veronica back, and everything will go on as planned." I peered up at Reese. "Right?"

He chewed the corner of his bottom lip. "You know this means we're dealing with potential terrorists, right? I need to call this in."

I grasped him by the arms. "You can't. You promised. The kidnappers said no cops. If they see Homeland Security roll in, they might harm the bride or Kate."

Reese frowned. "I don't like this. We should really get professional negotiators in here."

"You're a professional," I said, shaking his arms. "Anyway, you promised me you wouldn't tell anyone."

"That was before I knew the whole story. If I don't report a potential terror threat, I could lose my job."

"Please, Mike." I clutched his hands in mine and felt my eyes tear up again. "Just give me a little time."

He groaned as he met my eyes. "Fine, but I want to go on record for saying this is a bad idea."

"Mother of the bride at your six," Richard said, masking his words with a cough.

I turned around as Mrs. Hamilton stepped out of the French doors still wearing her long robe.

"Just the people I needed to see," she said, her eyes going from me to Fern to Richard and pausing when they reached Reese. "Who are you?"

Reese opened his mouth to speak but closed it again.

"This is Michael." Richard stood and patted Reese on the back. "My sommelier for the evening."

Mrs. Hamilton's eyes brightened. "I didn't know you brought a sommelier on-site. How lovely."

"Only for the special clients," Richard said. "The ones who truly appreciate fine wine."

The bride's mother gave Reese the once-over, her gaze lingering on the outline of his chest muscles through his T-shirt. "I've never met a sommelier who was so . . ."

Fern nudged her. "Isn't he though?"

"You know, my younger daughter is quite the wine connoisseur. You wouldn't happen to be single, would you?"

Before Reese could answer, Fern jumped in. "He's taken. Isn't it a tragedy?"

I felt my cheeks flush, and I took a small step away from Reese. It wouldn't take a genius to figure out we were together based on our body language, and it would seem unprofessional to have my boyfriend with me at work.

Fern cupped a hand to his mouth. "They're trying to keep it hush-hush, but Richard is ecstatic."

Richard's jaw dropped almost as much as mine did. I made a point not to look at Reese's reaction.

"I see." Mrs. Hamilton smiled as she looked from Reese to Richard. "Well, you two make a handsome couple."

Richard stammered and looked at his feet.

"Ready to finish your hair?" Fern asked the mother as he spun her around and propelled her into the house, craning his neck to blow a kiss to us.

"Don't look at me," I said as Richard shot daggers in my direction. "That was not what I had in mind."

He turned and stomped off, muttering as he went.

"Two minutes with your friends and I'm a gay wine expert?" Reese asked.

"I'm the one who should be upset," I said. "You're messing around with my best friend."

Reese gave me a side-eye glance. "It's going to be a long time before I find any of this funny."

CHAPTER 8

"Can you take me through the day so far?" Reese asked as he pulled out a chair for me at the kitchen table. "You know, before I need to go decant some wines with my boyfriend."

I tried not to grin as I sat down. "Again, I had nothing to do with that."

He rolled his eyes and took the seat next to mine. "Let's say you owe me one. A big one."

I felt my cheeks warm as I imagined the ways I could make it up to him. I absently picked up a blueberry muffin from the tray in the middle of the table and began peeling off the wrapper. I usually didn't eat the food set out during wedding setup, but I was starving, and the family and bridal party hadn't touched them. I figured most of the women were either off gluten, off sugar, or off breakfast pastries in general.

Reese pulled a small notebook from his back pocket. "Let's start with who's been coming and going from the house."

"More coming than going." I set down the unwrapped muffin and took the folded-up wedding day schedule from the pocket of my dress. "The tents were set up two days ago to make sure the ground stayed dry in case of rain. Then the flooring went in. They did the draping yesterday and came this morning to add the fans. Most of the guys left by noon, but one is scheduled to stay throughout the event."

"And that's normal?" he asked as he took notes.

"Pretty standard," I said, taking a small bite of muffin and catching the falling crumbs in my cupped hand. "We always keep one person on-site in case we need tweaks during the event. Kate and I don't want to be the ones on ladders adding sidewalls in the dark." I hesitated when I said Kate's name and heard my voice crack.

Reese stopped writing and looked up at me. "Don't worry. We'll get her back. Everything you're telling me will help me build a timeline of the day, and that will help me narrow down the people who might have done this."

I gathered my thoughts and took a breath. "Richard, Kate, and I were all here by nine o'clock this morning. The rental delivery was the first truck to arrive, and it dropped off right after nine and was gone by noon. Richard oversaw that since he placed the order. Buster and Mack came in next. They arrived on their Harleys and their setup team drove their box truck, which is still here."

"So none of the floral team has left?" Reese asked.

I shook my head and took another bite of muffin, tasting the sweetness of a blueberry. "Not that I know of. They wouldn't have any way to leave since they all came on the truck. Buster and Mack are still here and, as far as I know, so are their bikes."

"It would be pretty unusual for kidnappers to use Harleys as the getaway vehicles."

"They sure aren't quiet," I said, thinking of the loud rumbling noise that preceded Buster's and Mack's arrival. I would have remembered hearing that during the day.

Reese tapped his pen on the table. "Have any other vehicles left the premises?"

"I don't know. I've spent most of the day in the back of the house either setting up the ceremony tent or checking the reception tent. As far as I know, the gate wasn't guarded until after the bride disappeared. The Hamiltons usually buzz people in, and anyone could open the gates from the inside if they knew the location of the control panel. I've been buzzed in by their maids, the bride, and the mom's personal assistant before."

"So a vehicle could have arrived, been buzzed in, and left without alerting anyone?"

"Pretty much," I admitted, finishing the muffin and wiping the crumbs off my lips. "With all the setup craziness, I don't think anyone would have thought twice about another car or van driving up. The father of the bride's personal security team was much more focused on keeping eyes on him than on checking cars."

Reese flipped a page in his notebook. "Tell me about this security team. I think I saw one of them earlier."

"They're dressed in black so they blend in with the setup crews, but they're all packing heat. Apparently, the dad hired them after he got a big contract with the Department of Defense."

Reese raised an eyebrow. "What does he do again?"

"Pharma. He's been developing some sort of biotech weapon—poison gas, I think—and he'd gotten some threats on his life."

"By . . .?" Reese asked.

"No clue. I guess not everyone thinks it's a great thing to manufacture poisons used to kill people. The security team has definitely had eyes on the dad at all times. I get the feeling they're more muscle than brains since I haven't seen them doing much investigating since the bride disappeared. Aside from tightening security at the house."

"If they're ex-military, they aren't necessarily trained to investigate." He winked at me. "Unlike some people you know."

I wadded up the muffin wrapper, brushed the crumbs into one hand, and took them to the trash can disguised as a kitchen cabinet. "How does any of this information help us get Kate back safely?"

"I need to get a full picture of the day." Reese reached for a dark brown muffin I assumed was bran. "Tell me about the time right around the disappearance."

I sat back down and filled him in on Fern reporting the bride's cold feet, Kate going up to talk to her, and Fern reporting them both missing.

Reese tapped his pen on the table. "What time was that?"

"A little before three o'clock. It must not have been more than twenty minutes between when Kate went up and when Fern did."

"Plenty of time to get two women out the door and into a vehicle." Reese took a big bite of muffin, and a cascade of crumbs fell over the table.

"But why didn't they scream?" I asked, fighting the urge to sweep up the crumbs. "They would have had to pass right by the room where the bridesmaids were getting ready, down the stairs, and out the front door. There's plenty of time to call out for help or be seen during all of that."

"If they were held at gunpoint, they may have been too frightened to scream. Or they were convinced to go outside by someone they knew and trusted."

My stomach did a flip-flop, and I instantly regretted wolfing down the sugar-topped muffin. "You think the kidnapper was someone Veronica and Kate knew?"

"I'm only suggesting it as a possibility since you brought up a good question. How did no one see two adult women being taken from a busy house?"

I heard the footsteps before I saw the groom walking into the kitchen from the foyer. He was tall and slim with curly blond hair and wore a tuxedo but carried the jacket over one arm. Even though Tad had a name fit for the rich and famous, his unruly blond hair and tan skin always made me think he belonged on a surfboard.

I hadn't seen much of him during the setup, although I knew he was getting dressed in the bride's brother's bedroom. Did he know the bride was missing or were the bride's parents trying to spare him?

He ran a hand through his hair when he saw me. "So is this officially your biggest wedding day disaster or what?"

I guessed he knew. "Are you okay? Can I do anything for you?" I stood up and glanced around the room until my eyes landed on the tray of pastries. "Would you like a muffin?"

He didn't even look at the table. "I'm fine. I mean, I'm not fine. Of course I'm not fine." He leaned both palms against the marble counter. "How could I be fine? My fiancée is missing."

"I'm so sorry." I was especially sorry for the muffin comment. "I'm sure she'll be returned safely."

He sighed. "You have more faith in my future father-in-law than I do."

I noticed Reese shift in his chair, and I stepped in front of him. I didn't think the groom was paying much attention, but the fewer people I had to lie to about my boyfriend being a gay sommelier, the better. "You don't think Mr. Hamilton will do everything he can to get his daughter back?"

"Why did he put his family in danger in the first place?" Tad asked. "They were already filthy rich. His pharmaceutical company was huge. The family begged him not to go after the DOD contract, but he didn't care what anyone else thought. And now Veronica is paying the price."

I didn't know what to say. Over the years, I'd heard plenty of family members trash each other in front of me, and it was always uncomfortable and awkward. I couldn't take sides, especially when the bride's father was the one who was writing my check. "Why don't I get you something to drink?" I opened the industrial sized stainless steel refrigerator. "There's beer, wine, OJ."

"Water is fine." Tad draped his tux jacket across the counter. "Playing pool is more tiring than you'd think."

I remembered the billiards room from my exhaustive tour of the house during my first visit. I'd tried not to gape at the billiards room that looked like it had been lifted from the pages of a Regency novel and the movie theatre that could seat two dozen people in cushy leather recliners.

I took a bottle of water from the door of the fridge and passed it to him. "Was Veronica upset about the DOD contract?"

"She'd been distracted by the wedding planning," he said, unscrewing the plastic cap. "She hadn't really been herself for the past few weeks. You'd probably noticed."

I was so used to seemingly normal women losing their minds when they became brides that I didn't know if I even knew what constituted normal behavior anymore. "Wedding planning stresses everyone out." I knew the bride's cold feet were probably nothing, but I did wonder if there was a deeper reason for her sudden freak-out and desire to call off the wedding. "Had her stress been causing problems between you two?"

Tad's head jerked up. "Problems between us? Who told you that? Her mother?" He narrowed his eyes. "Or was it that sister?"

"No one said anything. It's not uncommon for couples to fight more close to the wedding, that's all."

His shoulders drooped. "Sorry. I guess I'm a bit high-strung myself." He took a swig of water. "The funny thing is, we hadn't been fighting about wedding stuff at all. It was the usual fights about her family."

I tried not to act surprised. I hadn't caught a whiff of this during the planning. Usually families loved to fill me in on all the bad blood and issues, but this was news to me. "She wasn't getting along with her family?"

He pointed a thumb at himself. "I'm the one who wasn't getting along with her family. They don't like me."

Again, this was news to me. I saw Reese making quiet notes as the groom spoke.

"Veronica is the princess of the family," Tad said. "I'm sure you picked up on that."

I'd actually thought everyone in the family behaved like they were royalty, but I kept that to myself.

"Since she's the oldest, she can do no wrong," he continued. "Except pick me. That is apparently the only mistake she's ever made. I'm not good enough for Veronica, and the entire family has made sure I know it. They've made things miserable for me. Well, except for her brother. Victor has been pretty cool. That's why I made him my best man. At least he's trying to take my mind off things by beating me at pool."

"Why get married if you're so miserable?" I asked.

Tad laughed as if this was the first time the thought had crossed his mind. "You know, that's an excellent question." He scooped his jacket off the counter and headed out of the room.

Had I just suggested to a groom that he call off his wedding? "I didn't mean . . .'" I began, but he was gone.

"Do you always try to talk your clients out of getting married?" Reese asked. "I think it would be bad for business."

"Who did you talk out of getting married?" Richard asked as he stepped in through the French doors leading outside. "I'm telling you, Annabelle, I can't take much more of this on-again, off-again business."

"Everything's fine," I lied. "This wedding is going to happen."

He put one hand on his hip and the other held a bottle of wine. "Without a bride?"

"We've done weddings without brides," I said.

"Yes, but there have at least been two grooms."

"There's always you and the detective," Fern said as he bustled into the room, hairbrush in one hand and champagne glass in the other.

Richard glared at him, spun on his heel, and went back outside in a huff.

I stole a glance at Reese who was not laughing. "Too soon?"

He flipped his notebook closed. "Years too soon, babe."

CHAPTER 9

"So what are you doing down here?" I asked Fern as he took the chair next to Reese.

Fern leaned back and let his arms flop to the sides. "I'm taking a break from the drama. I'm used to wedding day drama, but this is a whole new level. The bridesmaids are competing for who's more upset about Veronica being kidnapped."

"Crying?" I asked.

"None of them want to ruin their makeup or get puffy eyes, so they're trying to emote without actually shedding a tear. It's exhausting to watch."

"Have I ever told you what a strange job you have?" Reese asked. "And that's coming from a guy who deals with dead bodies on a regular basis."

I turned so that I could peer out the wall of windows overlooking the pool deck and the two tents set up for the cocktail reception and dinner. The security team was interspersed with the setup crews, and since both wore black, I had to squint to tell them apart. The blazers and gun bulges let me know I was looking at a member of the father's security team and not a lighting tech or sound technician. I wondered if the ex-military types were making any progress questioning people on-site or killing time until they got to shoot someone.

Reese stood up. "I have a good idea of the timeline of the day. Now I'd like to talk to the main players and see the last place the bride was seen before she disappeared."

Fern sat up straight and crossed his legs at the knee. "Ask me anything you'd like, Detective. I'm an open book." He paused and touched a hand to his throat. "Unless I'm a suspect. Am I a suspect?"

Reese grinned. "You're not a suspect."

"Whew." Fern slapped a hand to his leg. "I started to have a flashback to the time you tried to throw me in the pokey."

Reese mouthed "The pokey?" to me over Fern's head.

I raised both shoulders. Leave it to Fern to take his brief stint as a suspect and blow it into a traumatic life event worthy of PTSD. "Why don't I take you upstairs to the bride's room where she was getting ready?"

Fern popped to his feet so quickly he made me think of a jack-in-the-box. "I can give you the full dramatic crime reenactment."

Knowing Fern, dramatic was an understatement.

"A dramatic reenactment won't be necessary," Reese said, "but I would like to see the room for potential clues."

Fern's face fell.

I elbowed Reese. "But any details Fern might know would be helpful, right?"

"Of course," Reese said, and by his tone of voice, I knew he was humoring me. "You were one of the last people to see the bride before she went missing, so your information will be especially helpful."

Fern smiled and waved for us to follow him out of the room. "Veronica was upstairs all morning, from the time I arrived until she vanished. I never saw her set foot out of her room."

"Although we found Kate's phone on the floor by the door," I said as we passed through the marble foyer, motioning to the large double doors. "It stands to reason she and Veronica left by the front door, although if they were being taken against their will, I'm surprised neither yelled out. There are so many people around, someone would have heard them."

Fern paused as he reached the bottom step of the sweeping staircase. "But we were outside by the pool when Kate went inside to talk to Veronica, so we wouldn't have heard anything, and most of the setup is going on outside."

"True," I admitted as I put a hand on the mahogany banister, "but I still have a hard time believing no one saw them leave. All the bridesmaids were in the sister's room, and that's right down the hall."

"We should consider that the two women left of their own accord," Reese said.

I shook my head. "Even if Veronica was capable of doing something like this, Kate never would." I followed Fern up the curving stairs to the second floor and the large landing that divided into a hallway on each side. "Kate knows better than to take a bride off-site. Especially since she was in the limo with the bride who decided to drive around the block after I started the ceremony processional."

Fern turned and put both hands to his cheeks. "I remember that. One minute we were sending the bridesmaids down the aisle, then we turned around and the limo was gone with the bride in it."

"Do you remember how we had to tell the last two bridesmaids to walk very slowly?" I asked.

Fern giggled. "I remember watching you running around on the front lawn of the church looking for the limo. But that was better than watching those bridesmaids process herky-jerky down the aisle." He put a hand on Reese's arm. "I said 'step and together' but those floozies didn't listen to a word I said. It looked like they were in a bad Claymation movie the way they lurched toward the altar."

"Luckily, the limo looped the block and came back, but I lost a year off my life, and Kate got an earful," I said. "She wouldn't make that mistake again."

Fern directed us down one of the wide hallways to a room with a pair of white doors. He flung both doors open to reveal the massive bedroom complete with a sitting area and an en suite bathroom. "Voila. The bride's bedroom."

Reese stepped inside and swiveled his head to take in the space. "This is where she was the last time you saw her?"

Fern pointed to the vanity. "I had blown out her hair by the window. She liked getting to watch the setup from up here. We could see Annabelle walking around with her schedule out, Richard waving his arms at people, and the penguins in the pool."

Reese turned his head slowly toward me. "Penguins?"

"It's not as weird as it sounds," I said, gesturing to the stuffed animals on the bed. "The bride loves penguins. She's obsessed with them. It's the one thing she insisted on. Most of the other crazy ideas were her mom's, but the penguins were hers."

"Are we talking live penguins?" Reese asked.

Fern made a face. "Dead penguins would be creepy."

"Yes, they're alive. They're here for photos with the bride and groom and to circulate during cocktail hour so guests can see them."

Reese blinked at me a few times. "And you don't think this is unusual?"

"I think after planning weddings for so long, my threshold for unusual is incredibly high."

Reese shook his head as he turned back to Fern. "So it was you and the bride alone?"

"Oh no." Fern waved a hand. "People were in and out all day. Mostly her mother, who drove her crazy, but all the bridesmaids were in and out talking to her."

Reese walked the perimeter of the room, poking his head into the attached sitting nook with its overstuffed chaise lounge. "Anyone else?"

Fern tapped his finger on his chin. "Richard came up and brought nibbles sometime around midday, and a few waiters were back and forth with champagne."

I noticed the empty champagne flutes on the nightstand and the standing silver wine bucket by the vanity, beads of condensation on the outside telling me it had been there for a while.

"It doesn't look like there was a struggle," I said. Even though the room wasn't neat, it was no messier than most rooms were when brides got ready. Nothing had been knocked to the floor. Nothing was spilled or broken.

Reese inspected the bathroom, returning to the bedroom and putting his hands on his hips. "Very odd."

"What?" Fern and I both asked.

"You're right," he said. "You'd never know anyone was taken from this room against their will."

"So we're back to the theory that they weren't dragged out kicking and screaming?" I asked.

Reese held his hands out, palms up. "Well, if they were, they kicked in an orderly fashion and screamed so that no one heard a thing. Even if they were held at gunpoint, I'd expect some indication they were startled." He swept his arms open at the room. "Does anything look different to you?"

Fern's eyes swept the room. "Not a thing. She finished off her champagne glass, but that's not surprising since I left her to come downstairs and find you."

"Why did you need to find Annabelle?" Reese asked.

"To tell her the bride wanted to call off the wedding."

Reese arched one eyebrow. "Is that normal?"

"Brides and grooms get cold feet," I said, answering for Fern. "Kate's good with nervous brides, so I sent her up to talk to Veronica."

"I came back up a few minutes later, and they were both gone." Fern put his fingers to his lips and blew out a puff of air while fanning his fingers wide. "Vanished."

Reese took a few steps to the window and looked out. "So Kate either happened upon the kidnapping in progress, or it happened minutes after she arrived."

I swallowed hard, trying not to imagine either scenario and trying not to blame myself for sending her to talk to the bride.

Reese turned around. "I know you found Kate's phone, but what about the bride's? I'm assuming she has one."

"She was on it the entire time I did her hair," Fern said, taking a few steps over to the vanity. "It should be right here unless she still has it with her."

I felt a flutter of hope. "If she has it on her, we can locate the phone, can't we?"

Reese nodded. "Let's make sure it's on her before we do that. Can you call her? I'm assuming she's on speed dial?"

"No need. She called so often I just have to redial the last call received," I said, taking my phone out of my pocket. After I dialed, I heard a faint ringing coming from inside the room.

"It's here." Fern tilted his head as he took steps toward the sound.

We all followed the sound to the bed, where Reese dropped to his hands and knees and lifted the crisp white bed skirt. He held up the ringing phone as he stood.

I felt my shoulders slump. "So much for that plan." My eyes caught a flash of red by the corner of the bed, almost hidden behind the folds of the bed skirt. I picked up the single gummy bear, feeling my breath quicken as I examined the sticky candy covered in carpet lint.

"What's that?" Reese asked.

"Either the maid here isn't very thorough, or Kate left us a breadcrumb."

CHAPTER 10

*R*eese stared at the small red bear in my hand. "You think Kate dropped this as a clue?"

The initial confidence I'd felt when I saw the gummy bear wavered. "Yes. At least I think so. She may have done it to make us look under the bed."

"Where we found the phone," Reese added.

"She does always carry a packet of gummy bears on wedding days," Fern said, wrinkling his nose at the bear so covered in carpet fibers and dirt that it appeared to have a full head (and body) of hair. "She offered me one a few times earlier today."

"Okay." Reese moved his head up and down slowly. "Let's say she did drop this on purpose to lead us to the phone."

"That means she knew something was wrong before they left this room." My stomach clenched. "But for some reason, she couldn't call out for help or call me." I pulled out my phone, scrolling back to Kate's last message to me, the collection of letters unintelligible. "At least not in any way that made sense."

I held the screen out to Reese, who read it and put a hand on my arm. "You couldn't have known that was her attempt at a distress call."

"I know." I dropped my phone and the gummy bear into my pocket. Knowing didn't make me feel any better. "Do you think she left more clues?"

"Aside from her phone by the door?" Reese asked. "That was a pretty major one."

Fern dabbed at his eyes with the corner of his red scarf. "Such a clever girl, our Kate."

"But she might have dropped more before she was able to ditch her phone." I ran my eyes over the floor of the room, but didn't see any more spots of unnaturally bright color against the beige plush carpet. "She would have tried to do it subtly."

We shuffled out of the room as a group, taking tiny steps as we bent over and searched the floor. We baby-stepped our way down the hall and the staircase until we reached the front door. I opened one side, and we stepped outside and onto the large circular driveway. I heard the marble fountain before I could see it, the dancing cherub rising up from the center of the large round fountain and spouting water that splashed into the pool below. I looked down at the designer welcome mat. "This is where her phone was found."

"One question," Reese said, eyeing the fountain that looked as if it had been plucked from the streets of Rome, "did they base the Italian theme around the house, or did they redecorate the house to go with the wedding?"

"Not even my clients are crazy enough to remodel a house around a wedding," I said.

Fern sniffled. "I hate to think I must have missed them by seconds. I was probably walking from the kitchen when they were being taken out the front door."

"And you didn't hear a thing?" Reese asked.

"Who could hear anything over the opera singer rehearsing?" Fern asked, pantomiming putting his fingers in his ears.

"Before you say anything," I said, as Reese turned to me, "yes, we have an opera singer to serenade the guests during dinner and, yes, I know it's ridiculously over-the-top."

Reese grinned at me. "I like that you're starting to know what I think before I say anything."

"I don't care what Richard says." Fern whispered to me. "You and the detective aren't nausea inducing."

I hoped Reese hadn't heard that. I was used to Richard's snark, but Reese might take it personally to have someone say he induced vomiting.

"I don't see any gummies." I bent down to inspect the gray paving stones of the driveway and plucked a piece of white fluff from the ground.

"We're assuming she had any left," Fern said. "You know Kate loves her gummies. She might have eaten all but that red one before she was taken."

It was a good point. Kate munched on her gummies in proportion to the difficulty level of the wedding day, and with this wedding, I was surprised she'd had any left by noon.

Reese pointed to two small black orbs mounted over either side of the door. "Security cameras. We'll need to get the footage if they're recording and it's not just a live feed."

"I can ask Mrs. Hamilton's assistant," I said. "She knows everything house related."

"So no more clues?" Fern sighed.

I held up the white scrap of feather. "Unless you think she started molting."

Fern inspected it from multiple angles before shaking his head. "That's not even blonde. It's white, and thank heavens Kate hasn't started coloring her hair white. I'm all for trends, but why girls want to look like old ladies by dyeing their hair gray or white is beyond me."

"You have clients who want to go gray?" I asked, shoving the feather into my pocket along with the gummy bear.

Fern looked over his shoulder. "I don't like to talk about it. I made a name for myself making my clients look younger. This trend could ruin me. If one of my clients insists on doing it, I make them swear they won't tell a soul that I do their hair. Kind of like the agreement I have with you."

I touched a hand to my hair, which was pulled up into a high bun. "I've gotten a lot better about coming in for haircuts."

Fern crossed his arms over his black-and-white-striped chest. "Sweetie, you know I adore you, but hair maintenance is not where you shine. When do you *not* have your hair up in a bun or ponytail?"

I opened my mouth to protest, but closed it again when I realized he was right.

"I can name a few times," Reese said under his breath.

Fern's eyes widened in delight. "Well, well, well. Now this is getting interesting." Fern sidled up close to Reese. "Annabelle tells us nothing you know."

"I wonder why," Reese said.

Fern pressed a hand to his heart. "I hope you aren't implying that I would breathe a word to anyone." He lowered his voice. "I am the soul of discretion."

Reese did not look convinced. "Mmm-hmmm."

Reese had good reason to be suspicious. All of DC's best gossip passed through Fern's upscale Georgetown hair salon, sometimes passed along by Fern but, more often than not, made up by him. It wasn't unusual for his own gossip to circle back around and for him to have forgotten he made it up and be as shocked as anyone to hear it.

Before I could convince Fern there were no salacious details for him to ferret out, I heard the unmistakable sounds of creaking leather and heavy footsteps. I turned to see two massive stone urns approaching us from the side of the house with lush greenery and blooms bursting from the top and black leather-clad legs poking out of the bottom.

"It's like the S&M version of Birnam Wood approaching," I said as I watched Buster and Mack stagger toward us with the massive floral arrangements.

They made it to the front door where they lowered the urns onto empty pillars flanking the entrance, then backed up to assess the look.

"Were there always pillars on either side of the doors?" I asked, trying to remember from my many site visits.

"We brought them," Mack said. "They usually have topiaries."

I snapped my fingers. "That's right. The ones that are twisted into tall spirals."

"We moved those to the doors of the pool house," Buster said.

I stepped closer to the floral arrangement, reaching my hand out to touch a white plume arching from the top. "There are white feathers in a lot of the arrangements for today, aren't there?"

"White and black," Mack said. "To go with the masks."

I pulled the bit of feather from my pocket and tugged the gummy bear off of it, reminding myself to put them back in separate pockets. "Does this look like one of yours?"

Buster picked it up from my palm. "Could be, although it looks like this bit was pulled off a larger feather."

Mack leaned his head closer. "It's like the fuzzy bit of feather at the base. Where did you find it?"

"Out here on the ground. I thought maybe it came off one of the arrangements you brought inside."

Buster frowned. "If it is, our setup crew has some explaining to do. We've been loading in through the side all day so we wouldn't be traipsing through the house."

"Some of the performers have used the front door though," Mack said. "I saw one of them carrying an armful of feathered props."

Mack glanced at the gummy bear in my other hand. "I hope you aren't planning to eat that."

"No, it's one of Kate's. We found it on the floor upstairs. We thought maybe she left it as a clue."

Mack drew in his breath. "Like a trail."

"Exactly," Fern said.

"Did you find any more?" Buster asked.

I shook my head. "The phone outside the front door is the last trace of her."

Mack put a beefy arm around my shoulders. "We can help you search."

"I don't think we'll find any more physical evidence," Reese said. "From everything I can see, the kidnappers managed to get Kate and the bride out of here without being noticed or leaving behind much of a trace. Nothing was broken or damaged. Our only clues are two phones, one under the bed and one by the front door, and a gummy bear."

When he put it like that, our evidence didn't sound so impressive. I couldn't help feeling deflated. "So what do we do now?"

"Now we talk to people," he said.

"If you have anyone reluctant to talk, we can help with that." Buster folded his arms over his barrel chest, and I noticed his biceps bulge.

"You don't mean . . . ?" I'd never known my Christian biker friends to intentionally hurt a fly.

"We ask nicely and people tell us things you wouldn't believe," Mack said.

I wondered if he knew their intimidating presence made people spill their guts or if he genuinely believed it was their sparkling conversational skills.

Reese gave them both the once-over. "I may take you up on that."

"Anything to help get Kate back," Mack said. "As long as we don't break the Golden Rule or the Ten Commandments."

Reese gave a small shake of his head and looked at me. "Why does anything about your job surprise me?"

"I honestly have no idea."

CHAPTER 11

"So who do we interrogate first?" Fern asked as we walked back inside the house, leaving Buster and Mack to finish the front-of-the-house decor. Reese had promised to find them as soon as he had someone he wanted them to intimidate or pray over.

"I don't think we start with interrogation," I said.

We crossed the foyer as the sounds of the singing tenor wafted down the hall, and we entered the large open kitchen and casual dining area. I could see out the wall of windows that setup in the tent continued, although I no longer heard the band doing sound checks.

"Annabelle's right," Reese said, leaning both hands on the white-and-gray marble kitchen countertops. "We'll get better information if people don't know they're being questioned."

"You know," I said, "like the time we went to the drag queen's wake to talk to witnesses."

Reese drummed his fingers on the counter. "You mean the time you insisted you were at the wake to give condolences."

Fern elbowed me. "You still need to work on your subterfuge."

I felt my cheeks flush. "You get what I mean."

"Even though she's completely in the wrong, Annabelle is right," Reese said. "We want our conversations to be subtle."

Fern adjusted his red sash. "I can be subtle."

Reese hesitated briefly, no doubt wondering when Fern had ever been subtle. "I think we can all agree that Kate was not the intended target, so I want to focus on all the people connected to the victim. Especially the father, since his company seems to be the reason for the kidnapping in the first place."

"The bride's father is in his study," Fern said. "At least he was before we went upstairs."

"Perfect," I said, facing Reese. "You can talk to him and try to find out more about the ransom."

Reese tapped his pen to his lips. "I doubt he's going to talk to me. No police, remember? I'm not supposed to be here."

Fern snapped his fingers and crossed the room to the French doors leading outside. He opened one and leaned his head out. "Yoo hoo! Should we leave the lobster tails defrosting on the counter?"

I heard a shriek in the distance, then saw Richard hurrying toward us, hand waving. Fern backed up to let him into the kitchen.

"Lobster tails?" Richard said, his eyes darting around the kitchen. "Who brought lobster tails in here? What's going on?"

Fern put a hand on Richard's arm. "Good news first. There are no lobster tails defrosting. Bad news. We need you to go undercover with the detective to get information from the father of the bride."

Richard backed away from him. "Have you taken complete leave of your senses? What do you mean 'go undercover'?"

Fern crossed his arms over his black-and-white-striped shirt. "You did tell everyone Reese was your sommelier, right?"

Richard pressed his lips together.

"Of course." I clapped my hands together. "Fern, you're a genius!"

Fern fluttered his lashes at me. "Well of course I am, sweetie."

"You and Reese can have the dad taste tonight's wines. Hopefully, that will get him to open up." I looked from Richard to Reese, not feeling encouraged by either of their expressions.

Richard cocked one eyebrow. "You really think the bride's father will buy it? And proceed to spill his guts?"

"Crazier things have happened," I said.

"And usually to us," Fern added.

I took Richard's hand. "It could help us get Kate back safely."

Richard looked away from me as he let out his breath. "Fine." His eyes met Reese's for a moment. "Let me get the wines."

Richard left the room and Reese pulled me into a hug, planting a kiss on the top of my head. "You are the only person on the planet who could get me to pretend to be a wine expert in love with Richard."

I rested my head on his chest, comforted by how solid he felt. I breathed in his scent of soap and the faintest trace of aftershave. "I know." I wrapped my arms around him. "Thank you."

"While those two are off with the dad, what should we be doing?" Fern asked once I'd reluctantly pulled away from Reese.

"I, for one, want to know more about the groom," I said. "I may have Googled the bride's family since they were my clients, but I actually don't know much about the groom."

"Aside from the fact he's gorgeous?" Fern pretended to fan himself with his open palm.

"I want to know if it's true the bride's family doesn't like him and why. I feel like there must be a deeper story there."

"What's your plan for getting this info?" Reese asked.

I held up a finger. "There's one person in this house who knows all the dirt on everyone—the mother's personal assistant. She's been with the family for years."

Richard reappeared holding three bottles of wine against his chest and a wine opener in one hand. "Let's do this before I lose my nerve." He gave a cursory glance at Reese and strode across the kitchen in the direction of the father's study.

Reese met my eyes and ran a finger down the side of my face. "Be careful. There's a possibility someone on the inside was involved in this, and we still don't know who that is."

My pulse quickened at his touch. "I'll be fine."

"She's not the one I'm worried about," Fern said to Reese, rolling his eyes in the direction of Richard.

Richard glanced over his shoulder. "Coming, Romeo?"

Reese winked at me, and he followed Richard out of the room.

Fern watched them go. "Two men go into a study." He pantomimed playing an organ. "How many will emerge?"

"It won't be that bad," I said, although I wasn't so sure I believed my own words. "They aren't two peas in a pod, but they'll be fine."

"Two peas in a pod." Fern put a hand to his lips. "I miss the way Kate would have said it."

"You mean mangled?" I asked. Kate was notorious for mixing up expressions just enough to make you scratch your head and wonder if you'd gone a little crazy.

"Don't worry." I squeezed his shoulder. "She'll be back before you know it talking about two peas in a pond."

He began dabbing his eyes with the ends of the red scarf tied around his neck. "See? Doesn't that sound better?"

"If I'm going to talk to the mother's personal assistant, why don't you tackle the mother herself?" I asked.

Fern fluffed his red scarf. "She'll be a nice break from the bridesmaids."

"You don't think any of those girls have it in them to coordinate a kidnapping?" I said, remembering Reese saying the kidnappers might have had inside help and we couldn't rule out anyone. Technically, that included the bridal party.

Fern gave me the side-eye. "I wouldn't say they're a particularly loyal bunch, but I can't imagine why any of them would have the motivation. From what I can tell, they aren't a particularly socially conscious bunch. And political? Not unless there's an inauguration ball to attend."

I'd had limited contact with the bridal party so far, which was fine by me, but I agreed with Fern's assessment. Most of the bride's friends came from the same ritzy neighborhood or went to the same high-priced college. Kidnapping—unless it was for a surprise bachelorette party—wasn't their style.

Fern picked up his champagne glass and drained it. "Back to work."

Fern left the kitchen, and I headed down the hall to the assistant's office, knocking on the door before cracking it.

"You're back," Sherry said from across the desk where she sat in her black swivel chair. "Are you here to escape from the family or have a drink?"

I noticed the bottle of Jameson's still sitting on the corner of the desk. "Taking a breather from the drama." Not entirely untrue, although most of the drama was coming from my own team.

She motioned to the chair on my side of the desk. "Take Mrs. Hamilton's chair. That's where she sits when we go over the week's schedule."

"She stays busy, doesn't she?" I perched on the edge of the tufted chair.

Sherry leaned back and interlocked her hands behind her head. "Some weeks she's busier than her husband with all her volunteer positions and board meetings. Mrs. Hamilton likes to keep a packed schedule."

I thought back to the planning process and how challenging it had been to schedule meetings with her. Sherry and I had spent countless hours coordinating schedules so she could attend tastings and floral showings. I'd had an easier time setting up meetings with a bride who had been a top White House executive and on twenty-four-hour call to the president's chief of staff.

"Why do you think that is?" I asked. "It's not like she needs to do it."

Sherry eyed the whiskey. "I think the busier she is, the less she has to think about her life."

"I can't drink anymore, but don't let me stop you." I indicated the bottle with a tip of my head.

"Maybe a bit." Sherry filled one of the paper cups and took a drink. "You know I never used to drink before I came here to work. Well, not much at least."

"I've had clients who've driven me to drink before." I didn't tell her the wedding industry was filled with people who drank too much

71

because the difficult clients never stopped. "Do you think she's trying to take her mind off her marital problems with Mr. Hamilton?"

"That and all the problems with her children." Sherry's eyes went heavenward. "Of course if she spent more time at home, she might not have so many problems."

"Problems with her children? I thought Veronica and her brother and sister went to the best private schools around here and ran with the society crowd."

Sherry leaned forward. "That's the problem. Those rich kids run wild. Not to mention, none of the Hamilton children can stand each other."

I thought back to the brief interactions I'd had with Veronica's younger brother and sister. Had there been any bickering?

"The two younger ones think Veronica is the golden child, and they're jealous of all the attention she gets," Sherry said. "The wedding hasn't helped. Then there's the issue with the father's company."

"What issue?"

She refilled her cup. "I probably shouldn't be telling you this."

"This is between us," I said. "If anyone understands tough clients, it's me."

Sherry shuddered. "After dealing with Veronica during the wedding planning, I don't know how anyone can do what you do."

"Some days neither can I," I said, being completely honest.

"The bride's brother, Victor, was supposed to take over the company. Mr. Hamilton has talked for years about handing it down to his son, and Victor seemed eager to take over. That is, until Veronica graduated from college and couldn't find a job. She started working for her father and seems to have a knack for business. Now the old man's talking about handing the reins over to her or splitting it between the two."

"I take it Victor isn't thrilled about this?"

"Not by a long shot. He's accused Veronica of stealing the business from him. There have been some pretty big blowouts about it."

Could anger over a business translate to having your sister kidnapped?

"What about the youngest sister?"

"Val," Sherry said. "The one who gets overlooked the most. Mr. Hamilton never even considered giving her a part in the business. She isn't as power hungry as the other two, which means they sometimes forget about her and that makes her bitter, although she hasn't gotten in nearly as much trouble as the older two."

"I have a hard time imagining Veronica getting in trouble," I said. The bride struck me as type A.

Sherry laughed. "Remember how I mentioned the rough rich-kid crowd? Well, Veronica got in a little too deep with them and had to get straightened out. To give her credit, the stint in rehab really got her to clean up her act."

I nearly slipped off the edge of the chair. "The bride's been in rehab?"

"Where do you think she met the groom?"

CHAPTER 12

"The bride and groom met in a rehab facility?" I knew this was not the story they gave me when we first met, not that I would be eager to share that tidbit either.

"More of a rehab spa," Sherry said. "The bride went for alcohol, but I think the groom went for drugs, although nothing heavy."

This explained why the parents of the bride weren't crazy about their daughter's choice of fiancé. It also explained why an intense woman like Veronica would have selected a guy so different from herself. "So were the Hamiltons happy when their oldest daughter brought back a fiancé as a souvenir from rehab?"

Sherry snorted. "You should have heard the fights. Of course, that only made Veronica dig her heels in harder. She was always headstrong, and being told no never went over well with her."

"But her parents finally gave in or we wouldn't be here," I said. "I wonder if the bride had second thoughts earlier today."

Sherry tapped her paper cup on the desk. "What do you mean?"

I gave a shake of my head. "It doesn't matter now, but my hairdresser reported that the bride wanted to call off the wedding right before she went missing."

Sherry's mouth dropped open. "Does Mrs. Hamilton know? She'll be thrilled."

I thought it was an odd thing to say considering the circumstances. "Do you really think she cares about who her daughter marries at this point?"

Sherry's smirk vanished. "No, you're right. I'm sure all both parents want is to get her back. But the icing on the cake would be if she doesn't get married after all."

My mind went to the elaborate tents being set up to make guests feel like they'd been transported to Carnival in Venice, the five-course meal Richard had created to go with the Venetian theme, and the penguins frolicking in the pool. I did not imagine disassembling the entire production to be the happy end to this story. If Kate and Veronica were kidnapped and the wedding called off, I might need to stay in bed for a week.

"What's the groom's story?" I asked, noticing Sherry slumping further down in her office chair.

"Tad?" Sherry sat up straighter. "He's from California, which is enough to send Mr. Hamilton off the rails. He's convinced he's a hippie who'll convince Veronica to be more socially conscious and give all her money to charity."

That didn't sound so bad to me. There were probably better ways to spend half a million dollars than a lavish wedding, although I knew other people's over-the-top spending was the reason I had a job. "Is he?"

Sherry eyed the whiskey bottle but didn't reach for it. "He seemed like a nice enough kid to me. A lot nicer than the Hamilton kids, that's for sure. I've been dealing with those spoiled brats for years, and I'd take Tad over any one of them. He may not have come from a wealthy family or gone to an Ivy League school, but he was always nice to me."

"To me too."

Sherry held up a finger. "You can tell a lot about a person by the way they treat people who work for them. It's why you should never date someone who's mean to a waiter."

"That's what my assistant, Kate, always says." I heard my voice crack. "She has a lot more dating experience than I do, and that's one of her hard-and-fast rules."

"Smart girl. Is she the one who was taken along with Veronica?"

I nodded, the lump in my throat preventing me from speaking.

Sherry leaned over the desk and lowered her voice. "Can I give you some advice? Don't count on anyone in this house to care about your assistant. They may say they do, but this family only looks out for its own."

I took a few moments to digest this. "Are you saying they would let something happen to Kate?"

"Put it this way, honey. I've been working for them for over twenty years, and I wouldn't trust them as far as I could throw them." She splashed some whiskey into her paper cup and held the bottle out to me.

"Why do you keep working for them?" I asked, shaking my head at the offer.

"They pay me handsomely." She tossed back the drink. "Not every job would enable a single mom to send her child to private school and college, but this one has."

Knowing how expensive private schools in the DC area were, she wasn't kidding about being paid well. I glanced at a framed photo of Sherry with her arms around a young woman with bushy brown hair. "Is that your daughter?"

She smiled and her face changed entirely, the harsh lines around her mouth and eyes seeming to evaporate. "Stephanie makes it worth all the hassles."

Voices in the hallway prompted me to turn around as the door opened, and I recognized the pair of heads that appeared, along with a hint of hair spray and cigarette smoke.

"Oh, good," the bride's younger sister said when she spotted us. "One of you should be able to help us."

The few times I'd met her, Veronica's younger sister had struck me as a toned-down version of the bride. Shorter and less voluptuous with mousy brown hair, Val didn't have the presence of her big sister.

"Val," Sherry said with little enthusiasm. "What seems to be the problem?"

Val either didn't notice Sherry's nonplussed tone or didn't care. "We had to get away from my mother. She's being impossible." She jerked a thumb behind her to a girl with dark hair pulled into a French twist that I recognized as one of the cousins. "So Cara and I came down on a mission to find more chilled champagne."

I stood up. "I can locate that for you. Have you already gone through everything upstairs?"

Val made a pouty face. "My sister's college friends are lushes. Now they're all sitting around wailing about Veronica."

"Not that we aren't upset," Cara added, shaking her head.

"Speak for yourself." Val flipped her hair off her shoulders. "I'm telling you, this is another one of Veronica's stunts. She has to have all the attention, and what could get more attention than faking your own kidnapping?"

Cara's cheeks flushed, and she seemed embarrassed by her cousin's wild accusation. "Why would she need more attention? She's already a bride."

Val rolled her eyes. "To a guy everyone hates. Now that our parents decided to go along with it, she realized she didn't want to marry the guy in the first place, so instead of calling off the wedding, she pretends to be kidnapped."

I looked at Sherry to see what she thought of this theory, and her expression told me she thought it was as farfetched as I did. "Even if Veronica decided to stage her own kidnapping, which I don't think she did, my assistant would never go along with it."

Val hesitated. "I forgot that the blond girl is missing too."

I tried to keep my voice even. "That blond girl is my assistant, and she would never do something like this to terrify people."

Val didn't meet my eyes. "Well if this is real, I feel sorry for your assistant. My father may love Veronica the most, but he loves his money and reputation more. If they're counting on him to save the day, they're screwed."

We all watched as she stalked off down the hall.

"I should apologize for my cousin," Cara said. "Emotions are running a little high, and she's had too much to drink."

"It's not your fault," I said. "And I'm sure Val is more worried about her sister than she's letting on."

Sherry made a noise behind me that told me she wasn't so sure, but I ignored it.

"And don't believe all the bad things she says about her father." Cara looked over her shoulder. "Val has issues with him because she's convinced Veronica is his favorite, but Uncle Stephen isn't as bad as she makes him out to be."

"Do you still want me to find some champagne?" I asked.

Cara laughed. "Probably not the best idea. I may try to scrounge up some coffee for Val."

"Check with the catering staff in the garage," I said, gesturing to the door at the end of the hall leading to the makeshift garage kitchen. "They may have the coffee pots plugged in by now."

"Thanks," she said as she stepped out of the room.

"So not all the family is high-maintenance," I said, turning around to face Sherry.

"Because she wasn't raised by the Hamiltons," Sherry said. "She's the only daughter of Mrs. Hamilton's sister. Cara didn't grow up indulged like her cousin since *her* mother didn't marry into money."

"So Mrs. Hamilton didn't come from money?"

"Not by a long shot. You've heard the expression 'the wrong side of the tracks'?"

I thought back to the old woman I'd met earlier who'd claimed to be Mrs. Hamilton's mother. If it was true the bride's mother came from a different class, the old lady would make sense. "I did meet the grandmother earlier."

Sherry rolled her eyes. "Mrs. Hamilton does her best to keep her mother at arm's length. I can count on one hand the number of times she's visited in all the years I've been here."

"I can understand why."

"Can't you though?" Sherry shook her head. "You have to give it to Deborah. She's done an amazing job of creating her new persona and distancing herself from her trashy family. You'd never guess she had any connection to them."

"But Cara seems nice. Not rough around the edges like her grandmother."

"She's had the advantage of the Hamilton money without being spoiled rotten like the Hamilton kids. Can you keep a secret?" Sherry asked, lowering her voice, but not waiting for me to reply. "Mrs. Hamilton sends her sister money every month. From what I've seen, her mother and sister make her feel guilty for leaving and striking it rich with her husband."

"She only sends money to the sister?" I asked. "Not her mother?"

"She bought her mother a house. Granted, it's somewhere in the Midwest, so it cost peanuts compared to houses around here."

"Does Mr. Hamilton know?" I asked, wondering what a man so concerned with amassing wealth would think about bankrolling extended family.

"I can't say." Sherry spread her palms wide on top of the wooden desk. "I do know the Hamilton children don't know, which is a good thing for Cara. I doubt they'd be as fond of their cousin if they knew she was inadvertently dipping into their future inheritance."

"You don't paint a pretty picture of the Hamilton siblings."

Sherry held her palms open and swept them wide. "They're a product of all this. I don't think they had much of a chance to turn out selfless."

"There's a big difference between selfless and cold-hearted. Veronica's sister seemed callous about the whole situation."

Sherry sat forward. "And you haven't even met the brother yet."

I realized the difficulty was not going to be finding people motivated to get rid of Veronica. The tough part would be finding people who weren't.

I stood to leave, then remembered one of the reasons I'd come to talk to her. "Are the security cameras over the front door live feed only or do they record?"

Sherry's eyes shifted down. "I wondered when that might come up."

"What? Are the cameras fake?" I knew some businesses put up fake cameras to scare off potential robbers, but I couldn't imagine the Hamiltons cheaping out on security when the father had hired a private team.

"They aren't fake," Sherry said. "They just haven't been recording for a few weeks."

I waited for a beat before prodding the woman. "Why?"

Sherry blew out her breath. "I suppose it's going to come out at some point, but Mrs. Hamilton had me turn them off so there wouldn't be evidence."

I felt my pulse quicken. Was Mrs. Hamilton somehow involved in her own daughter's kidnapping? "Evidence of what?"

"Of her affair with Mr. Hamilton's business rival and her best friend's husband, Tarek Nammour."

CHAPTER 13

"*D*o you think it's too much?" Alexandra stood back from the towering wedding cake and assessed the flowers Buster and Mack were attaching to the front of the rolling cake table.

The cake itself stood five tiers high with a cushion of tightly packed white roses between the tiers. Each tier mimicked one of the elaborate designs from Carnival masks—a multicolored diamond pattern on the large bottom tier, crimson with gilded leaves above it, black and gold swirls covering the next layer, glittering blue accents on the penultimate tier, and the top layer covered in iridescent gold fondant and imbedded with jewels. A duo of Venetian masks made of sugar and exquisitely detailed with metallic rope and feathers perched on the top in lieu of a traditional bride and groom figurine.

Buster straightened up from where he bent over attaching a curtain of white orchids extending from the base of the cake down the tablecloth to the floor. "I thought the whole theme of the wedding was 'too much.'"

"He's right," I said as I joined them in the kitchen. "If the opera singer, footman, and doge to welcome guests aren't too much, I doubt the cake will put it over the top."

I was still reeling from everything I'd learned from Sherry, but I wanted to digest the information and what it might mean before sharing it with everyone. Focusing on wedding prep would be the perfect way to distract my overwhelmed mind.

"Annabelle!" Alexandra rushed up to me and enveloped me in a hug. "The boys brought me up to speed. I'm so distraught about our dear Kate."

I inhaled her familiar scent of sugar mixed with expensive perfume. "Thanks, but we're going to get her back. And the bride."

Alexandra pulled back. "Of course I'm worried about Vanessa as well."

"Veronica," I corrected.

"Right. Her too." Alexandra turned her attention back to the cake. "Do you think Van—I mean Veronica, will like it?"

"It's exactly what she described and what you sketched out. I think it's perfect."

Alexandra let out a whoosh of breath. "The one drawback of living in Scotland and flying back to DC to do cakes is I don't get to know the brides."

"Isn't that also the reason you moved to Scotland?" I said. "So you wouldn't have to interact with brides."

She winked at me. "I didn't say it was a drawback I minded."

"So what's the verdict on the tablecloth of orchids?" Mack asked, holding a spray of phalaenopsis orchids in one hand.

I appraised the cascading white orchids. "The clients want lush, and this is lush. I think they'll love it."

Buster began attaching the blooms again, but Mack came over to me. "Is there anything we can do to help get Kate back. Aside from the obvious?"

I knew for Buster and Mack the obvious was praying, while for me the obvious was poking around where I probably shouldn't. I put an arm around his shoulders, but my own arm only reached halfway across his back. "The best thing we can do now is prepare for the wedding as if nothing is wrong. Chances are good the dad will pay the ransom, and the bride and Kate will be back here in plenty of time for this wedding to happen."

Mack raised a pierced eyebrow. "Are you sure the bride will want to get married after being kidnapped?"

I knew my desire to act as if everything was normal was more for myself than anything, but I also knew if we didn't keep busy, we'd go crazy with worry. "I've always said it takes a lot to stop a bride. We've had weddings in the immediate aftermath of hurricanes and during code orange terror warnings, remember?"

"Those aren't my best work memories," Buster said, his voice little more than a gravelly rumble.

"But we got through it together." I squeezed Mack. "The same way we'll get through this. We may need to push things back a bit time-wise, but I'll bet the bride will be happy to have a celebration after her ordeal."

I knew if Kate was with me, she'd say I was letting my need to fix every problem get the better of me. I missed having her be the devil's advocate and sassy counterpoint to my arguments.

"You really are the iron fist in the velvet glove, aren't you?" Mack said. "I don't know what we'd do if you weren't holding us all together."

"You know what you can do?" I said. "Keep your eyes and ears open for anything that seems out of the ordinary."

Since I knew the security cameras wouldn't give us any information, we were back to gathering clues the way we'd always done—snooping and prying.

Mack's eyes shone. "Do you mean spy?"

Buster pulled himself up to his full height. "We've never gone incognito before."

Considering both men were well over six feet tall and topped three hundred pounds, all covered in black leather, this was not surprising.

"Not spying per se, but the more we know about the dynamics around here, the better. And someone had to have seen something when Veronica and Kate disappeared, but they may not know they saw something important."

Mack stroked his dark-red goatee. "So you need us to interrogate witnesses?"

"Not interrogate," I said quickly. "Just pay attention to what people are saying and how they're reacting. I already discovered the bride's sister thinks Veronica is staging this entire thing to get attention."

Alexandra shook her head. "I wouldn't put anything past a bride these days."

"Even if the bride was crazy enough to stage a kidnapping for attention, Kate would never go along with it," I said.

"Of course she wouldn't." Mack put a hand to his mouth. "The kidnapping must be real. Oh, our poor Katie."

"None of that," I said, feeling my eyes water. "We can't help Kate if we're upset."

"You're absolutely right." Mack sniffed and squared his shoulders. "You can count on us to be an extra set of eyes and ears."

"Two extra sets," Buster added.

"Don't forget me," Alexandra said. "I can be quite persuasive when I want to be. Are there any men we need to question?"

I started to tell her no, then I remembered how men reacted to the beautiful baker. "Actually, there are plenty of men around here I'd love to know more about."

She undid her high ponytail and let her chestnut brown hair spill across her shoulders. "Point me in the right direction."

"There are three men in the immediate family: the bride's father, her brother, and her fiancé. I think the fiancé is harmless, although I think he's in way over his head with this family. Reese and Richard are supposed to be talking to the father, although I'm afraid to know how that's going."

"Leaving the bride's brother," Alexandra said. "What's his story?"

"I don't know much about him except what the mother's personal assistant mentioned. She doesn't seem to think much of him, although she doesn't have a high opinion of any of the Hamilton kids. According to her, there's no love lost between the siblings. I do know the brother is supposed to take over his father's business, so he might have a vested interest in how this ransom will affect the company."

"Any idea where he might be?" Alexandra asked.

"Actually, yes." I snapped my fingers. "The groom was playing pool with him in the billiards room a little while ago. They're probably still there."

"The billiards room?" Alexandra's perfectly arched brows arched higher.

"It looks just like it sounds." I pointed behind her. "Go down the long hall off the foyer and past the living room, study, and library."

"Fair warning," I told her as she headed across the large room. "If the groom is still with him, you'll be getting two for the price of one."

Alexandra waved a hand over one shoulder. "Nothing I can't handle."

Mack nudged me once she'd left the room. "I'm glad she's on our side. She can be a little intimidating."

Buster nodded. "Like a black widow spider that eats the male after mating with him."

I opened my mouth to disagree with them, but found their description more fitting than I'd have liked to admit. I was used to Kate's lighthearted flirting, but Alexandra definitely gave off a more sultry and seductive vibe. I suspected most men didn't stand a chance against her exotic beauty and practiced charms.

"But she's *our* black widow," I finally said.

"I hope she knows not to seduce the groom," Mack said. "The last thing we need is to get the bride back and have him call off the wedding because he thinks he's in love with the cake baker."

"She knows better than that," I said before stopping to think about it. "At least I think she does."

Buster crossed his arms over his burly chest. "You sure?"

"I'd better clarify," I said, heading toward the doorway she'd disappeared through.

"Good luck," Mack called after me.

I walked as quickly as I could without breaking into a run, passing the living room with its vaulted ceiling. Before I reached the study, a woman stepped into the hall, and I nearly collided with her.

"Where's the fire, hon?" The middle-aged woman with curly brown hair took a step back from me.

Something about the woman rang a bell. "Sorry. I'm the wedding planner, Annabelle Archer."

Her shoulders relaxed. "My sister has talked about you. Good things." She held out a hand. "I'm the bride's aunt, Connie."

No wonder she looked familiar. She had the same blue eyes as the mother of the bride, although she looked older and clearly hadn't had the advantage of expensive skin care and Botox. Luckily for Aunt Connie, she didn't look as weathered as her mother. "How is your sister doing?"

"She's beside herself, and her husband is worthless, as usual."

I tried not to show my surprise at her harsh words for her brother-in-law, especially as I remembered what Sherry had told me about the sister and how Mrs. Hamilton had been secretly sending her money for years. If she felt any gratitude for the Hamilton money, she hid it well.

"You don't think Mr. Hamilton is doing everything possible to save his daughter?" I asked.

She crossed her arms tightly across her chest, pushing up her sun-damaged cleavage so I had to make a point to avert my eyes. "I think if he has a choice between saving himself or saving his family, he'll pick himself every time."

This was not what I wanted to hear. If the father didn't pay the ransom, not only was Veronica in danger, so was Kate. I knew for the Hamiltons my assistant was an afterthought, but she wasn't for me. "I hope you're wrong. My assistant was taken too."

Aunt Connie pressed her lips together as she backed away. "I'm real sorry for you. I hope for your sake the lying sack of manure comes through this time."

She left me with my mouth hanging open and more questions that needed answers. I forced myself to keep going down the hall, knowing I still needed to find Alexandra and warn her off seducing anyone. I paused as I drew even with the open door to the father's study.

"Of course I know who's behind all this," the father of the bride's voice carried out to the hall. "He's even a guest at the wedding."

CHAPTER 14

I peered into the study, my eyes adjusting to the darker woods and richer colors of the room. From the crack in the door, I could see the massive wooden desk carved with an intricate scrollwork pattern and one of the walls of shelves. A thick Persian rug in shades of burgundy and gold covered the floor, and I saw two pairs of legs facing the desk. I recognized Richard's beige pants and Reese's jeans, but I did not see a third pair. The father of the bride must be sitting behind the desk.

"The kidnapper is a guest at your daughter's wedding?" Reese asked, his voice carrying out of the room.

I pressed my back against the wall and edged my ear closer to the crack in the door, making a conscious effort to quiet my breathing. The last thing I wanted was to be caught snooping.

"I didn't say he kidnapped Veronica," Mr. Hamilton said. "Did I say that? Well, I didn't mean that exactly. What I meant was this never would have happened if my competitors hadn't made so much noise about me winning the DOD contract."

"Which competitor?" Reese asked.

"You wouldn't know the name unless you know about the pharmaceutical industry. Aren't you a sommelier?"

"Yes, he is," Richard said. "Why don't you try this Pinot Noir? It's assertive without being pushy and has a hint of cherry in the finish."

I heard the sound of wine being poured into a glass, and I tilted my head to get a better look. As I suspected, Mr. Hamilton sat in his wingback leather chair with several wine glasses lined up in front of him. His attention was focused on the red wine he swirled in a crystal goblet so he didn't see me, but I saw enough to recognize the full head of dark hair and relatively unlined face.

My encounters with him during the wedding planning had been brief, but I'd been struck by how young he looked for a father of the bride. He didn't have the receding hairline or middle-age paunch most fathers of a certain age claimed. Instead, he had thick, wavy brown hair, a trim waist, and the golden skin of a frequent golfer or someone who frequented a tanning bed. I suspected the former.

"I like it, but I shouldn't be talking about wine at a time like this."

"Your wife has insisted we carry on with the wedding plans because Veronica will be back in time," Richard said. "We don't want to make her angry."

Mr. Hamilton laughed, but there was no mirth in it. "No, we don't. I suppose she's right. We need to keep ourselves in the mindset that our daughter will be back home soon."

"All you have to do is pay the ransom, right?" Reese asked.

The father hesitated. "In theory. The reality of procuring the ransom is more complicated."

"Oh?" Reese prodded.

"I shouldn't talk about it. Not until it's finalized and my assistant has procured it for me to deliver. We should probably get back to the wines." He took another drink. "We're serving this one on the bar or with dinner?"

"On the bar," Richard said at the precise moment Reese said, "With dinner."

"We can do both is what we mean," Richard said, and I saw him shoot Reese a look.

"My wife mentioned you two are a couple." He gestured to

Richard and Reese, and I noticed both men shift. "I think that's great. Live and let live, am I right?"

"Yes, sir," Richard said, but I could tell he was biting back the urge to deny his fake relationship with my boyfriend.

"Are you planning to get married?" Mr. Hamilton asked. "Since you can?"

"No," both men said emphatically.

The father's eyes widened at the strong reactions. "Too early? I get it. If you ask me, my daughter rushed into this marriage. I don't know why everyone's in such a hurry. They've got their whole lives to be miserable." He threw his head back and laughed.

Richard and Reese both laughed politely, but I could tell Richard was seething at the indignity of pretending to be involved with a straight man like Reese. Not to mention, a straight man he didn't like in the first place. I knew that although Reese was definitely handsome, he wasn't nearly stylish or coiffed enough for Richard's taste.

"What do you think about the Pinot?" Mr. Hamilton asked when he'd stopped laughing at his own joke. "You're the expert after all."

Reese glanced quickly at Richard. "I'd agree with Richard. It's offensive without being mushy."

Richard groaned as the father scratched his head. "He means metaphorically. The palette isn't muddled."

The father took another swallow. "I see what you mean." He set the glass of Pinot Noir back on the desk. "Don't we have the Cabernet Sauvignon for dinner?"

"We did have the Cab to go with the rack of lamb," Richard leaned forward with a second bottle and poured some in a glass. "Why don't you try it again?"

I jerked my head back as the father looked up and reached for the new glass.

"I probably shouldn't drink too much. My wife is already livid at me. If she thinks I'm drinking when I should be out saving our daughter, she'll take me to the cleaners."

"This isn't drinking," Richard said. "This is wine tasting. Your wife can't be upset at you for trying to make sure the wedding is perfect."

"If there is a wedding," Mr. Hamilton's voice slurred slightly.

"Once Veronica is back, I'm sure we can proceed as planned," Richard said.

I heard Mr. Hamilton give a deep sigh. "If I get her back. It's not as simple as it sounds." He lowered his voice. "Between us, the kidnappers are asking for some of the nerve agent my company has developed, not money. That's why it's taking so long to get it."

I put my eye to the crack in the door as Richard refilled the father's glass. "This is more full-bodied with jammy flavors and a hint of clove."

"And this is a problem?" Reese asked.

Mr. Hamilton took a gulp. He was clearly past the wine-tasting stage and fully into self-medicating. "I've been developing this product for the government. If I give it to the kidnappers, not only is it treason, it's probably terrorism. I could go to prison, and my company would be destroyed."

"Who do you think would want to get their hands on the nerve agent?" Reese asked.

Mr. Hamilton leaned back in his chair, closing his eyes. "Any number of fringe terrorist organizations, not to mention the countries who conduct chemical warfare. I wouldn't even know how to narrow the list."

Reese rocked back on his heels. "And the project wasn't secret?"

Mr. Hamilton opened his eyes. "It was supposed to be, but like I said, my competitors made a big stink about me winning the contract. They claim I used political influence, but who doesn't these days? I'm convinced they were the ones that leaked information about what I was developing. It's no secret now what we were working on and that we've finalized the formula and made it stable."

"Why would they do that?" Reese asked while Richard topped off the father's glass.

"To make me look bad." The father raked a hand through his hair. "I still don't know how they found out what they did, but this project has been consumed by leaks from the start. And now this." He blinked a few times and focused on Reese. "What did you say about this wine again?"

Reese paused. "It's full-bodied and hammy."

I could hear Richard's sharp exhale.

The father smacked his lips. "You know, I think I can taste the ham."

"I must be losing my mind," Richard muttered.

"And you said one of your competitors will be at the wedding?" Reese asked.

"Tarek Nammour of NK Enterprises." He grimaced as he said the name. "We run in the same social circles and our wives are friends. My wife insisted on them being on the guest list."

I slapped a hand over my mouth to keep myself from gasping out loud. Tarek Nammour was the name of the man Sherry said Mrs. Hamilton was having an affair with. Was it possible her lover was involved with the kidnapping, and did that mean Mrs. Hamilton was as well? I couldn't believe the bride's mother would harm her own child, but truth be told, I didn't know her well, and the secrets in the Hamilton family seemed to be piling up pretty high.

"Why don't you take a sip of the Pinot again?" Richard suggested, glaring at Reese. "To get rid of the ham flavor."

"You think he would be involved in kidnapping your daughter?" Reese asked, ignoring Richard's stare.

Mr. Hamilton balled his fists, opening and closing them several times, then slumped back in his chair. "I think he'd love to see my company go down in flames, but I doubt even he would do something this despicable. Not when our children have grown up together."

A line of men wearing floor-length velvet cloaks the color of Merlot, white masks, and velvet hats paraded by me. I recognized them as part of our path of masks that would line the footpath leading guests from the ceremony to the reception. When the bride had added the twenty additional costumed attendants, we'd already been well past the point of overkill, but seeing them in an ominous row reminded me what a spectacle we were producing. Dismantling this wedding would take almost as much effort as assembling it had.

The troupe was dressed early, so I was glad I could cross that off my checklist, although men in white pointed masks and head-to-toe velvet parading through the house did give me pause. Sidney Allen had insisted it would add to the romantic Venetian atmosphere. I thought they were seriously creepy. I tried to act casual as the masked men marched by. I crossed one leg over the other and leaned back against the wall as if I'd merely stopped in the hall for a rest.

When they passed, I twisted around so I could peek into the study again.

The father held up a glass of red wine. "Definitely the Cabernet for dinner, but I'd like to put it on the bar for after dinner as well."

"Excellent decision." Richard gave a slight bow of his head. "Some guests will want to continue enjoying it afterward." He lowered his voice. "Despite the ham aftertaste."

"We ordered several microbrews for the bar, didn't we?" Mr. Hamilton asked. "My son and his friends don't have an appreciation for wine yet, but they like their beers to be expensive."

"A few of the best," Richard said. "Will the younger men drink wine with dinner?"

"Who knows?" The father waved a hand in the air. "These boys don't seem to want to grow up. My son was supposed to take over my company, but he's more interested in socializing than working. Would you believe Veronica is the one with the head for business? And she has a better nose for wines." He put his head in his hands. "Not only did they kidnap my oldest daughter, but they kidnapped the incoming CEO."

It took me a moment to unravel what he meant.

"Your daughter will be taking over the reins of your business?" Reese asked.

Mr. Hamilton didn't look up. "We signed the papers this morning. I was going to announce it tonight at the wedding."

CHAPTER 15

*R*ichard gave a high-pitched yelp as he nearly bumped into me leaving the father's study. "Good heavens, Annabelle. What on earth are you doing out here?"

I put a hand over his mouth and pulled the door closed so the father wouldn't hear us. "Keep it down. I'm obviously listening in on your conversation with Mr. Hamilton. Did I hear correctly? Veronica is the new CEO?"

Reese led us a few steps away from the door. "That's what he said, which means our pool of suspects just widened."

Richard mumbled something underneath the hand I still held across his mouth.

I dropped my hand. "What was that?"

"Is there some sort of tariff on hand cream I don't know about?" He wiped at his mouth. "Your skin is like sandpaper, darling."

"I'll add it to my to-do list," I said. "Right after finding Kate and salvaging this wedding."

Richard twisted to face Reese. "Remind me never to ask you to pick out the wine. When have you ever heard of a wine being hammy?"

Reese shrugged. "There are all sorts of odd flavors used to

describe wine—earthy, buttery, grassy. I thought you said hammy, and I didn't think it was so farfetched. Maybe next time don't make me a sommelier."

We all stopped talking as a pair of jesters wandered past us dressed in black-and-red costumes with ruffled collars and hats sprouting points of stiff fabric tipped with bells. Bells hung from their long tunics and adorned the tips of their shoes, making the performers jingle with each step.

"Next time?" Richard touched his fingertips to his throat once the jesters were out of earshot and the jingling had faded. "I certainly hope your going undercover at our weddings doesn't become a habit."

"You think this is fun for me?" Reese narrowed his eyes at Richard. "I'm not here ten minutes before I'm outed and dating an older man."

"Older?" Richard's voice was no more than a hiss. "Did you refer to me as an 'older man'?"

I cringed. Richard may have been significantly closer to forty than I was, but it was something we never discussed. Just like I pretended not to notice we were in a Groundhog Day loop when it came to celebrating his thirty-fifth birthday.

I put a hand on Richard's arm as he began to stagger back against the wall. "He didn't mean older as in age, did you?" I glared at Reese. "He meant older as in more sophisticated and worldly."

"Sure," Reese said. "That's what I meant. Older as in a finely-aged wine."

"Don't push it," I muttered. "If you call him hammy, I'll kill you."

Richard's breathing returned to normal. "I've always thought of myself as a precocious Syrah bursting with fruity undertones."

"Sounds about right," I said, ignoring the look from Richard and turning my attention to Reese. "I heard what the dad said about the rival he blames for spilling the secrets about his DOD project."

"Tarek something-or-other," Richard said.

I motioned for them both to follow me further away from the study door. "Tarek Nammour. The same guy Mrs. Hamilton's assistant says she's been having an affair with."

Richard made a face. "Sherry's been having an affair with Mr. Hamilton's business rival? How tacky."

"Not Sherry," I said. "Mrs. Hamilton. That's why she had the security cameras turned off. So there wouldn't be video record of him coming over."

"So the cameras out front?" Reese asked.

"Useless," I told him. "Sherry says they haven't been recording for a few weeks."

"So this Tarek Nammour is the husband's top business rival and is sleeping with his wife?" Richard said. "Oh, the wicked weaves we web."

I cocked my head at him. "I beg your pardon?"

"What can I say?" Richard said. "I've gotten used to Kate's mangled expressions."

I pivoted to face Reese. "Do you think that gives Tarek Nammour a motive? Or does it implicate the mother?"

Reese ran a hand through his dark hair, and the single curl that fell over his forehead dropped back into place. "It's too early to know. It seems like this Tarek guy may have had a reason to hate Hamilton. Getting a government contract is big money, and if the dad beat out his competitors by cheating, they could have tens of millions of reasons to want him to suffer. At first glance, it makes sense that whoever is demanding the poison gas is a terrorist, but what if the goal isn't to use the gas but to tank the company making it?"

"So one of his rivals gets Hamilton to violate his contract and break the law. The rival then has the chance to step in when Hamilton's arrested or fired?"

"Maybe they get the contract," Reese said. "Maybe they humiliate him and ruin him financially. Maybe they devalue his company enough to buy it. If it really is this rival Tarek, maybe it has to do with the fact that the man is sleeping with Mrs. Hamilton. It could be a double whammy. Ruin your rival and steal his wife. Win-win."

Richard pretended to shiver. "That's cold."

"But believable," I said. "Wouldn't you be out for revenge if a fellow caterer stole one of your signature recipes?"

"I'd strangle them in their sleep," Richard said.

Reese's eyes widened. "I'm going to pretend like I didn't hear that."

"But if the guy is sleeping with Mrs. Hamilton, isn't he already getting his revenge?" Richard asked. "Chances are the leaks Mr. Hamilton mentioned are coming from his wife indulging in pillow talk. Tarek Nammour is already doing damage. Isn't it overkill to kidnap his rival's daughter and destroy his company?"

"Maybe," I said. "Either way, he'll be here in a couple of hours, and we can question him."

"Don't forget the bride's brother." Reese held up a finger. "If he found out his father was turning over the reins of the company to his sister, he could have had plenty of motivation to try to eliminate her."

"But wouldn't he be damaging the company he wants to run? You don't bite the hand that feeds you." Richard frowned.

"You mean 'don't bite the head that feeds you'?" I asked, channeling my inner Kate to properly mangle the expression. "Or bite the hand that feels you?"

Richard let out a small sigh. "Now it feels right."

"Maybe," Reese answered, "but revenge isn't always logical. We also don't know what the brother knows. The bride being named CEO could have been a surprise to him as well."

"I can tell you it wasn't," Alexandra said, sauntering toward us from the end of the hall as she pulled her hair up into a ponytail, her scent of sugar and perfume reaching me before she did.

I noticed her skirt looked twisted, and I regretted getting distracted on my way to specify that she wasn't to seduce anyone in her quest for information. "You found the bride's brother?"

"Oh, yes." She winked at us as she linked her arm through Richard's. "I had a lovely chat with the boy. Such a doll."

This didn't sync with how Mrs. Hamilton's assistant had described him. "Victor?" I said. "Tall? Dark hair?"

She nodded. "All he needed was a little attention to get him to open up."

I did not want to know what kind of attention she gave him. "And he told you he knew his sister was going to be made CEO?"

"He overheard his father talking to her. The poor boy was crushed after thinking for years he would follow in his father's footsteps."

"His father's footsteps might be leading to jail," I said. "So maybe he dodged a bullet. Do you think he had anything to do with his sister's kidnapping?"

Alexandra glanced over her shoulder. "To be honest, I don't think the boy has the initiative or ingenuity to pull it off. He's not terribly fond of either sister, but I don't think he's clever enough to hatch a plan and coordinate a team."

"I don't think we can eliminate him yet," Reese said. "I'm not discounting your intuition, but we need to fully consider everyone until we can eliminate them definitively."

Richard's phone trilled and he pulled it out of his jacket pocket, letting out an exasperated breath when he saw the name on the screen. "Yes, Leatrice. What is it?"

Reese gave me a questioning look.

"Leatrice is watching Hermes for him," I whispered. "She's had a lot of questions."

"No, you cannot color his hair," Richard said, tapping his foot in rapid-fire against the hardwood floor. "I don't care if it washes out. I do not want a pink dog."

Reese grinned. "A pink dog might suit him."

Richard inhaled quickly as he listened, and I wondered if we were approaching breathing-into-a-paper-bag territory. "Absolutely not! I don't care if perms are making a comeback. If I don't get my dog back looking exactly like he did when I dropped him off, heads will roll."

I took the cell phone from Richard. "Hey, Leatrice. It's Annabelle."

"Hello, dear. Can you tell Richard he's being no fun?" Hermes yipped in the background.

"How about you go with non-permanent accessories?" I suggested. "You know they have feathers and colored hair you can clip right into your regular hair? They even have clip-in bangs."

Richard reached for the phone. "No feathers and no bangs!"

I stepped out of his reach. "As long as it's removable, you should be fine."

"What a wonderful idea, dear," Leatrice said. "Maybe I'll try feathers too. Hermes and I can match. I guess we're off to the beauty supply store."

I hung up and handed the phone back to Richard, trying not to laugh as I imagined his face when he saw his Yorkie and my octogenarian neighbor in matching hair feathers. "Problem solved."

"Are you out of your mind?" Richard asked, dropping his phone back into his pocket. "You authorized Leatrice to buy my dog a hairpiece. If Hermes has a comb-over when I pick him up, I'm not speaking to you for as long as I live."

We paused our conversation as a pair of enormous masked performers approached in burgundy velvet cloaks and shiny white masks with elongated noses and chins. These two would certainly make a statement as part of the "row of masks" greeting arriving guests.

I waited for them to pass so I could start talking again, but they stopped when they reached us. "Are you looking for the rest of the greeters?" I asked, shifting in place as they stared at me from behind their blank masks.

"It's us." Mack's deep voice took me by surprise as he and Buster pulled off their masks.

I gaped at them. "What are you doing?"

"We're incognito." Buster replaced his mask on his face, and I wondered if his motorcycle goggles were tucked under his black velvet hat.

"Why?" Richard asked.

"There are so many performers and vendors on-site, there's a chance one of them is either involved in the kidnapping or saw something but is afraid to say something," Mack explained. "So we're infiltrating. We figure there's a better chance of someone talking if they think we're one of them."

"That's not the worst idea," Reese said.

Since the two men were noticeably larger than every other masked performer, I wondered just how incognito they would be.

"Do *not* let Sidney Allen see you." The entertainment diva would have a coronary if he saw two linebacker-sized performers with leather pants poking out of the bottom of their costumes.

"Is he the high-strung fellow with the clipboard and headset?" Buster asked.

"And the pants devouring his body inch by inch?" Richard said. "That's him."

Mack slipped his mask back on his face. "With that in mind, we'd better run before he sees us."

The two men lumbered down the hall away from us, their capes flapping around their black leather calves instead of reaching their feet.

"Are those capes supposed to be high waters?" Alexandra asked.

Richard draped a hand over his eyes. "My life is a Fellini film."

CHAPTER 16

*J*led everyone down to the ceremony tent because it was far enough away from the house that no one could overhear us, and it was shaded so we wouldn't get sunstroke while we talked.

"This is pretty," Alexandra said as she took in the rows of folding chairs and the enormous gilded frame at the altar area flanked by two towering arrangements of white blooming branches and feathers. Since the tent was open on all sides, the view through the frame was of the rolling hills, the horses out to pasture, and the wooden barn in the distance. "Less fussy than the reception tent."

"Guests will only be here for thirty minutes, so we tied the decor into the theme but used the natural landscape as the focus," I said, taking a seat on the front row and picking up a feathered fan.

She winked at me. "You sound like Buster and Mack."

"I guess all the years of listening to them describing floral decor has rubbed off." I fanned my face to keep the beads of sweat that were forming around my hairline from trickling down my forehead.

"Do we think it's a good idea those two are doing our undercover work?" Richard asked, sitting next to me with his back ramrod straight and not a drop of sweat in sight.

"I'm not sure how undercover they actually are," Reese said.

Richard gave him a quick glance. "Exactly my thoughts."

"Great minds think alike." Reese took the seat on the other side of me and draped an arm across the back of my chair.

"Well," Richard sniffed as he scooted closer to me, "don't let it go to your head."

I took out my wedding day schedule and flipped it over to write on. "If every crime is based on motive and opportunity, why don't we figure out who has one or both from what we know so far?"

Reese leaned over and whispered in my ear, "Are you trying to turn me on by talking like this?"

I elbowed him, hoping Richard wouldn't hear and stomp off in a tizzy. I wanted to build on their moment of detente instead of reminding Richard of the ways he couldn't compete with my boyfriend.

"You want me to Google all the terrorist organizations in the world?" Richard asked, producing his phone.

"Even if a terrorist organization orchestrated this, they didn't burst in wearing ski masks and brandishing machine guns," Reese said, flipping open his own notebook. "This was done with stealth, which makes me think the people involved were either on-site as part of the setup crew or were pretending to be. And we shouldn't assume a terrorist group is behind the kidnapping simply because of the ransom. No group has claimed responsibility. I'm still not convinced the ransom isn't a distraction to make us think this is terrorism when it may be corporate warfare."

Richard rubbed his chin. "You believe the father's claims?"

"I think he knows better than any of us what producing this ransom will do to his company and to him. It's a clever way to strike at him without actually taking a shot at him, especially since he beefed up his personal security. This man felt threatened enough to hire a bunch of paramilitary guys to watch him like a hawk. We have to take that into consideration."

"We should also remember what we know about Mr. Hamilton. If he's the target, who hates him enough to pull a stunt like this to get even with him?" I said. "From what I can tell, it's a lot of people. And plenty of them are related to him."

Alexandra meandered to the altar area and stepped through the giant frame. "His son is pretty hurt about being cut out of the CEO job, but I don't get the feeling he'd kidnap his sister to get back at his father."

"The bride's Aunt Connie had some choice words about her brother-in-law, but she also seems close to her sister. Even if you think your sister's husband is a 'heaping pile of horse manure,'" I made air quotes, "you don't kidnap your niece to stick it to him."

"Heaping pile of horse manure?" Richard said. "I feel like I might like this Aunt Connie."

"She's the same one Sherry told me was secretly being sent money every month by the mother," I said. "So this family clearly has some issues."

"Sherry?" Alexandra asked.

"The mother's personal assistant," I explained. "She knows everything. She's the one who told me the bride and groom met at rehab, and the mother has been supporting her side of the family with her husband's money for years."

Reese scratched in his notebook. "I wonder what other secrets this Sherry knows. I should probably talk to her."

"Does she know the bride's mother is planning on asking for a divorce?"

We all turned around to see Fern striding down the aisle from the back of the tent.

"What?" I stood and let Fern sink into my empty chair.

"It's true," he said, taking the feathered program from me and fanning his face. "She was only waiting until after the wedding so she wouldn't steal her daughter's thunder."

"When were you planning on telling us?" Richard asked.

Fern snapped his fan shut and rapped it on Richard's leg. "I just found out when I was taking the curlers out of her hair, but it took forever to find you all. Do you know how long it takes to search every room in that house?"

"Who else knows about this?" Reese asked. "Does the father?"

"Not from what I could understand." Fern unfurled the feathered program and resumed fanning himself. "Annabelle, sweetie, would you be a dear and get me some lemonade? I'm feeling a bit light-headed from my ordeal."

"Ordeal?" Richard rolled his eyes. "You walked down a hill."

I knew Richard hated anyone else to be more dramatic than him. Usually, it wasn't an issue.

"Of course." I headed down the aisle to the lemonade station. "But don't say anything else until I'm back."

I filled a champagne flute with raspberry lemonade from the large glass container, then decided to fill another for myself. The glasses were cool in my hands, and my mouth watered as I looked at the pale-pink liquid. I hurried back up the aisle and handed Fern one of the glasses.

Richard took the other. "You read my mind, darling."

So much for quenching my thirst. "So Mrs. Hamilton told you all this as you were doing her hair?"

Fern drained half his glass. "She and her sister were talking while I finished her hair. To be honest, I think they forgot I was there. It happens a lot."

I knew what he meant. It wasn't unusual for clients to forget that waiters, hairdressers, and staff had ears. If we were around enough, we became part of the furniture to them. I'd heard plenty of juicy tidbits during wedding setup, especially when champagne was involved.

"Was she drinking?" I asked. Fern had been known to take the edge off his clients by either getting them or himself drunk.

He bit his bottom lip. "She might have taken a teeny sedative to calm her nerves, but I don't think it was anything she hadn't taken before."

"Who could blame her?" Alexandra said.

She made a good point. Most doctors would probably prescribe a sedative to a mother whose daughter had been kidnapped, so I couldn't quibble with that.

"So she was planning on asking for a divorce," I prodded. "Did it sound like this was a reaction to the kidnapping or something she'd been thinking about for a while?"

"I'd say the latter since she's already met with an attorney."

"What do you think this means?" I asked Reese.

"The bride's father is even less popular than we thought," Richard answered for him.

"He's right," Reese said. "So many people have an issue with Mr. Hamilton, I think we really need to give more credence to the theory that this kidnapping is actually meant to hurt him."

Richard gave me a smug smile. "See? I'm right."

I narrowed my eyes at Reese. If he was trying to win over Richard, it seemed to be working, although I wasn't sure I could handle a more self-important version of Richard.

I made a list of names on the back of my wedding day schedule. "The people we know dislike Mr. Hamilton are his wife, his son, his younger daughter, his sister-in-law, the groom, his mother-in-law, and an untold number of corporate rivals, including one who's a guest at the wedding."

"So the only family member who does like him is currently missing because she's been kidnapped?" Alexandra made a tsk-ing noise in the back of her throat. "Bad luck for him."

"Good thinking," I said. "Another way to hurt the dad. Target his favorite child—the only family member who likes him."

Richard made a face. "Ugh."

"You disagree?" I asked.

"No." Richard motioned for me to look behind me. "Ugh, here comes Sidney Allen."

I turned to see the egg-shaped man making his way down the hill toward us, his face flushed from the exertion as he barked orders into his headset.

"Bless his heart," Fern said. "One false step and he's rolling the rest of the way down."

I could tell Sidney's Southern speech had started to rub off on Fern, who was already a bit of a chameleon.

"Who's Sidney Allen?" Reese asked, watching the small man wind-mill his arms to keep from falling.

"He's an entertainment designer," I said.

Reese tilted his head at me. "A what?"

"He designs the entertainment and coordinates all the various performers."

"That's actually a job?" Reese gave a quick shake of his head. "I don't think I'll ever understand the wedding industry."

"What's up, Sidney Allen?" I asked, walking forward to meet the man as he reached the tent.

"Theft, that's what's up." He stepped into the shade and began fanning himself with his clipboard.

"Someone mugged you?" From his seat, Fern shook his head slowly. "What is this wedding coming to?"

"For heaven's sake, I wasn't mugged." Sidney Allen threw his clipboard down onto the grass. "My costumes were stolen."

I thought of Buster and Mack wandering around in capes and masks. "Are you sure someone didn't misplace one or two or maybe borrow them?"

Sidney Allen's eyes looked as if they might pop out of his head. "Who borrows embroidered doge capes?"

"Doge capes? You mean the white ones with all the beading and feathers?" I asked. "You aren't missing robes for your path of masks?"

Sidney Allen heaved his pants up a few inches. "The burgundy ones? Not that I know of. Why did you assume those were missing?" He tapped his earpiece. "Columbina Two. Can you count the costumes for the path of masks?"

"No reason," I said, cringing as I saw Buster and Mack appear from the house and rush past the pool, barreling down the hill toward us, the long burgundy robes flapping behind them and their masks in their hands. The ground vibrated as they got closer.

Sidney Allen turned in time to see Mack trip on the velvet cloak and stumble forward, catching himself with his hands and rolling head over heels into the last few rows of chairs. I dodged out of the way as the wooden chairs crunched beneath his girth and scattered across the grass, but Sidney Allen was not so lucky.

"My costumes!" he screamed as Mack knocked into him, sending him skidding across the grass face-first.

Buster had slowed his descent of the hill and held his robe up with both hands as he jogged the last few feet. Reese went over to check on Sidney Allen, rocking him back and forth a few times to get him upright, while I checked on Mack.

"Are you okay?" I leaned over the burly florist as he lay on his back, looking up and breathing heavy.

"Thank heavens we found you," he said, his chest heaving.

"They're wearing my costumes," Sidney Allen squeaked from where he leaned against Reese, grass stains running from his face down to his pants, and his headset bent so the microphone nearly went up his nose.

"What's going on?" I asked as Buster reached us.

"I'll tell you what's going on." Sidney took an unsteady step toward the two men. "These two hooligans stole my costumes."

Buster ignored Sidney Allen as he leaned his hands on his knees and caught his breath. "We found a dead body."

CHAPTER 17

$\mathcal{M}$y skin went cold, and I felt my knees weaken. "Who? Who is it?"

"We don't know," Mack said as he struggled to his feet. "A woman neither of us recognized."

I almost cried with relief. For a moment, I'd expected them to tell me they'd found Kate. I allowed myself a deep breath, pushing down the taste of bile that had forced its way into my throat.

Richard sank into a chair at the back of the aisle. "Another dead body at a wedding?" He draped a hand over his forehead. "I don't know how much more of this I can take."

"Another dead body?" Sidney Allen gaped at us. "How many are there?"

Fern patted his arm. "This is the first one so far today, sweetie."

Sidney Allen did not look comforted as he tried to unbend his headpiece and take a few steps away from us. "All teams report in," he said into his mangled microphone, his voice shrill. "Columbinas? Pulcinellas? Harlequins?"

"I've never been on-site when you've found a body," Alexandra said, sitting down next to Richard. "I don't know what to feel, but this is a shock."

"Shock is a good way to describe how to feel," I said. Perhaps I should have gotten used to dead bodies, but I still felt a visceral reaction at the thought of a person being killed—my palms were clammy, I felt light-headed, and my throat had gone dry.

Richard lowered his arm. "Was the victim dressed like one of my waiters? I can't afford to lose any staff. I could barely get enough waiters to cover this event."

I glared at Richard, and Alexandra swatted his leg.

"Not that I'm not upset someone was killed," he mumbled.

"First a kidnapping and now a murder?" Fern's eyes took in our group. "At least we know it wasn't one of us. I don't think I can handle losing another."

"We haven't lost Kate," I said, my voice louder than I'd intended.

Alexandra took my hand. "Of course we haven't."

"Thank heavens," Sidney Allen said as he rejoined our group. "It wasn't one of my performers."

"Where is the victim?" Reese asked, his face serious. "I need to find out who was killed, so I can figure out what it has to do with the kidnapping."

"Kidnapping?" Sidney Allen's face paled again under the bright-green grass stains.

"Sorry, Sidney," I said, not succeeding in making my voice sound sincere. "The bride and my assistant were kidnapped earlier today. We had to keep it on the down low."

He opened and closed his mouth like a fish gasping for water.

Buster jerked his head in the direction of the house. "Inside."

"Okay." Reese began taking long strides out of the tent and up the hill to the house as the rest of us scurried behind him, except Sidney Allen, who seemed frozen to his spot under the tent. "Who else knows about this?"

"You're the first people we've told," Mack said, puffing as he climbed the hill.

I wiped the sweat from my forehead, wishing I wasn't wearing all black, even though it was by far the most practical color for working a wedding.

"But someone may have heard us when we found the body and ran around looking for you," Buster admitted, cutting his eyes to Mack. "It was a bit of a shock."

It didn't take much imagination to know there might have been some shrieking on Mack's part, as he was the more demonstrative of the pair. I gave a cursory glance at the reception tent as we reached the pool deck—setup continued with waiters bustling around tables and musicians setting up on the stage. If the victim was one of the setup crew, the remaining staff clearly had no idea.

"Lead the way." Reese held open one of the French doors leading into the kitchen for Buster and Mack to step through.

Buster took off his black velvet hat to reveal his flushed bald head and the motorcycle goggles still perched on top. "As you know, we were trying to blend in with the performers and see if they knew anything about the kidnapping."

"Any luck?" I asked, following Alexandra into the air-conditioned house and feeling instantly cooler.

"They must be method actors, because most of them have taken their silent roles seriously and won't utter a word." Mack shrugged off his cape and hung it over the back of a kitchen chair. "Especially the masked performers. The jesters were chattier, but none of them saw anything. Everyone we spoke to claimed to have been changing in the pool house earlier in the day."

"That's their green room," I explained. "Since there are so many of them, we have food and drinks set out so they don't have to bother Richard, and we don't have to worry about when to feed them. They can grab snacks anytime they want instead of all of them taking a meal break together and leaving us with no performers."

"How many performers are hired for this wedding?" Reese asked once we'd all come inside and Fern had closed the door behind us.

I thought for a second. "Between the masked greeters, the doge and his footmen, the jesters, the opera singer, the acrobats, the stilt walkers, the lute trio, and the gondoliers there must be about fifty."

Reese gave a low whistle. "Is that normal?"

Fern sidled up next to him and patted his shoulder. "It's a wedding, sweetie. Normal is a relative term."

"This way." Mack beckoned for us to follow him through the kitchen and down the hall toward the garage.

We traipsed behind him single file until we reached a door. My stomach clenched when Mack stopped and opened the door to Sherry's office. I pushed Richard and Alexandra aside and rushed into the room, gasping when I saw the blond woman lying on the floor of her office.

Reese grabbed my arm before I could go any further. "Stay here. I don't want you disturbing the crime scene."

He scanned the small room before leaning over the body and crouching down beside her.

"Do you know her?" Buster asked.

I leaned against him to steady myself. "This was Mrs. Hamilton's personal assistant, Sherry."

"The one who told you all the dirt?" Alexandra asked.

"That's the one."

Fern sucked in air. "You don't think she was killed because of what she told you, do you?"

"Or what she hadn't told you yet," Richard added.

I didn't look at either of them. I couldn't take my eyes off the woman who'd been so chatty and had been tossing back whiskey with me less than an hour ago. Aside from a red bump on her forehead, she didn't look too different from when she'd been alive.

I turned when I heard a cry from the doorway. "Is that Sherry?"

Val and Cara, the bride's sister and cousin, had pushed their way through our group and stood with their mouths open in the doorway.

I shook myself out of my stupor and tried to turn them around. "Everything is under control, ladies. Why don't we go into the kitchen?"

Val shook me off. "Is she . . .?"

"No, she's not," Reese said from the floor.

"What?" We all said together.

"She's been knocked unconscious." Reese looked around, taking his fingers from the side of Sherry's neck. "But she's alive and her heartbeat is steady."

"We should call 911." Richard pulled out his phone and began dialing.

I snatched his phone out of his hand. "If we call the paramedics, what happens to Veronica and Kate? What if the kidnappers see the fire truck and ambulance and freak out?"

"Are you suggesting we don't get this poor woman help?" Mack blinked at me.

"I can help." The bride's brother pushed his way through the group. "I was pre-med for a year."

Reese eyed him, but let Victor join him kneeling next to the motionless woman.

Val bit the edge of her thumbnail. "He's the only one of us who doesn't get sick at the sight of blood."

Victor gave his sister a look over his shoulder. "No blood here. It looks like she was hit on the front of the head, but not hard enough to kill her."

Buster released a breath. "So we don't need to call the paramedics?"

Victor stood. "She'll be fine."

Cara looked at Sherry, then at Victor before saying under her breath, "Someone should stay with her until she's conscious and put an ice pack on her head to reduce the swelling."

Reese raised an eyebrow at the woman.

"My mom's a nurse," she said by way of explanation. "You pick up things."

Victor's face darkened, and he muttered as he left the room.

Cara knelt beside Reese. "I'm happy to keep an eye on her."

"You heard the woman," Reese said. "Ice pack."

"I'll get it," Richard said, rushing off and returning a minute later. He handed Reese an ice pack with a blue-striped dish towel tucked perfectly around it. Leave it to Richard to give an ice pack military corners. Sherry moaned as Cara touched the ice to her head.

"That's a good sign," Cara said, smiling at us.

"Thank heavens," Richard said. "I don't know if I could have handled another dead body at one of our weddings."

I pulled him a few feet away from the group and into the hallway. "It doesn't bother you the woman who told me all the dirt on the Hamiltons was attacked? Even if they didn't succeed, someone tried to eliminate her."

Richard's eyes grew large. "I didn't think of it that way."

Reese joined us, looking up from his phone where he'd been tapping. "I'm really not comfortable with this, Annabelle."

"I'm sorry I dragged you into this mess," I said. "I know this isn't how you wanted to spend your day off."

"You think I'm upset about my day off?" He shook his head at me. "I'm not sorry I'm here. You all need all the help you can get. I don't know how much longer I can go without calling in rein-forcements."

My eyes darted to Sherry sprawled out on the floor. "Do you think she was attacked because she talked to me?"

"That woman talked to everyone," the grandmother said as she approached us from the other end of the hallway. "You weren't nothing special."

I stared at her. "Your daughter's assistant has been attacked. Someone tried to kill her."

An expression I didn't recognize crossed the gray-haired woman's face. She held a highball glass with a few melting ice cubes circling the bottom and swirled them before she took a drink. "Sherry knew more than was good for her and didn't know when to keep her mouth shut. I warned my daughter about her. Not that she listened to me."

"You're saying Sherry deserved to be attacked?" I asked.

"Now I didn't say that, girlie. Just that I'm not surprised it happened. When you know where the bodies are buried, and you're responsible for a few skeletons yourself, you better watch your back, that's all." She shuffled off in the other direction, leaving me with my mouth gaping open.

"What do you think she meant by that?" Richard asked.

"Clearly it was no secret that Sherry knew a lot about the family," Reese said. "Did anything she told you implicate someone?"

I thought about it. Although she'd given me some inside dirt, nothing was worth killing over. "Not really. And nothing I haven't told you already."

"It might have been something she *didn't* tell you."

"So someone wanted to make sure she never got the chance to spill the real secrets?" I asked.

Richard clutched my arm. "If that's true, then the person is still running free."

I put a hand over Richard's and looked Reese in the eyes. "Which means we need to find out who wanted to silence Sherry and what all this has to do with the kidnapping before someone actually gets killed."

CHAPTER 18

"*We* should call in the cops," Reese said, stepping further down the hallway.

"I already did," I said as I followed him. "You're not telling me your colleagues would do a better job than you, are you?"

The door at the end of the hall opened, giving me a peek into the bustling garage-turned-catering-kitchen and sending a cloud of savory smells wafting into the house. Several chefs in white jackets stood chopping and slicing at long tables, while waiters in long bistro aprons filled water pitchers and bread baskets. A waiter poked his head inside, saw the crowd in the hallway, and closed the door again.

Reese narrowed his eyes at me. "Nicely played, babe, but you know I can only do so much working outside the system."

I glared at him. "Even if more cops means Kate could be killed?"

Richard pushed his way through the crowd in the doorway and joined us in the hall. "I think I'm developing late-onset claustrophobia."

"I wouldn't call this house a small, confined space," I said.

Richard shot a look at the people gathered around Sherry in the office. "What do you call the syndrome where being around people for more than two minutes annoys you?"

"Being Richard?" I suggested.

He cocked one eyebrow at me. "Hilarious." He looked from Reese to me. "Am I interrupting a lover's spat?"

"I was telling Annabelle I need to call in reinforcements, especially since there's been an attempted murder," Reese said.

"And I think any more law enforcement puts Kate at risk," I explained.

Richard studied us both for a minute, arching a perfectly coifed brow before pivoting to face me. "You know I'm not a big fan of us playing detective, darling." He held up a hand before I could argue. "But I also know you'd never get over it if anything happened to Kate."

Reese let out a burst of breath. "I'm trying to save Kate, but I honestly don't know if I can do it on my own."

"You're not on your own," I said, throwing an arm around Richard's shoulders. "You've got us. Not to mention Fern, Buster, Mack, and Alexandra."

"None of you are trained investigators," Reese said.

"But we have been involved in more than a few criminal investigations," I argued. "And we've helped you nab murderers."

Reese did not look convinced.

Richard looked over his shoulder into Sherry's office and headed toward the kitchen door. "Let's take a break from the drama."

"I think we'd have to leave the metropolitan area to do that," I said as the three of us proceeded to the kitchen. "Between the wedding, the kidnapping, and the attempted murder, this is drama central."

"Attempted murder?"

I hadn't noticed the mother of the bride, but her voice made me turn to see her sitting at the long kitchen table beside her sister. The women wore robes and held mugs in front of them with what I hoped was coffee.

My mouth fell open as I tried to figure out a way to break the news to Mrs. Hamilton about her assistant.

"There's been an accident," Richard said, stepping forward when I clammed up.

Aunt Connie eyed us. "She said attempted murder."

"We don't know for sure." I made my way around the kitchen island, gathering empty glasses out of habit as I went. "Sherry was found unconscious in her office."

Mrs. Hamilton leapt to her feet. "Sherry? My assistant?" She clutched her hands in front of her. "It must have been an accident. Why would anyone want to hurt Sherry?"

"You sure she didn't pass out?" the grandmother asked, walking into the room.

Mrs. Hamilton shot her mother a look. "Where is she?"

Aunt Connie stood up. "I'll come. I might be able to help."

Their mother jerked a thumb in Connie's direction. "She's a trained nurse. Comes in handy, although she can't write prescriptions or give you notes to carry your emotional support gopher on an airplane." She guffawed at her own joke.

Mrs. Hamilton pressed her lips together, obviously fighting the urge to snap at her mother.

"Mom, please," Aunt Connie said in a warning tone, but her mother continued laughing.

"Your daughter is helping her now," I told the aunt. "They're in Sherry's office."

Mrs. Hamilton pulled her robe together in the front as she rushed out of the room toward her assistant's office with her sister close behind her. Their mother took a seat at the kitchen table and pulled one of the abandoned coffee cups in front of her.

"You don't look worried," I said as I watched the grandmother lean back and stretch her legs out in front of her.

The gray-haired woman twitched one shoulder. "These are rich people problems. Maybe if my son-in-law wasn't so greedy they wouldn't be in this mess."

Reese slid out a chair across from her. "You think this is all because of money?"

"What else? Doesn't all crime have to do with sex or money?" She leaned forward, giving him a cross between a smile and a leer.

"Are my eyes playing tricks on me, or is granny moving in on your man?" Richard whispered.

I gave him an exasperated look, and he gave me one back of pure innocence.

"What? You have to watch out for cougars these days," he said so only I could hear. "Although, even on your worst day, you don't have to worry too much about this one."

"Thanks," I said. "I think."

Mrs. Hamilton's mother turned her attention to me and Richard, waving her hand at us. "You two are thick as thieves. Are you a thing?"

"Bite your tongue," Richard said.

"Again, thanks," I said to him, catching Reese turning around and grinning at me.

"Money might explain the kidnapping, but what about someone attempting to kill Sherry?" I asked, trying to steer the conversation back to the crimes.

The grandmother slapped her hand on the table. "Why does my daughter need a personal assistant? You tell me that. It's not like she's got a job, unless you count going to lunch or attending fundraisers a job."

I knew many wealthy women in the DC area did consider those things their profession, but I didn't point that out.

"She's always been too big for her britches," the woman continued. "That's her problem. Thinks she's better than everyone else. Well, what she's got isn't so great if you ask me."

"I've heard she's been pretty generous with you and her sister." I knew I shouldn't say anything, but I felt like someone needed to defend my client when she wasn't there to do it.

The grandmother eyed me. "You did, did you? She used the word generous?"

Before I could answer, Mr. Hamilton entered the room. He wore tuxedo pants and a shirt open at the collar with a bow tie hanging loose around his neck. He froze when he saw his mother-in-law at the table.

"There's the big man himself," Mrs. Hamilton's mother said.

"I'm really not in the mood right now, Candace." He made his way to the refrigerator where he reached in and took out a bottle of water. "All I care about is getting my daughter back, so you can save your snide remarks for someone who cares."

"Snap," Richard said, his expression telling me that the father had moved up a few notches in his estimation.

"Far be it from me to criticize," the grandmother said, arching a painted-on eyebrow. "I'm glad to see you concerned about one of your children. It's a nice change."

I realized I was holding my breath as I watched Mr. Hamilton and his mother-in-law stare each other down from across the room.

"Stephen, there you are." Mrs. Hamilton rushed into the room from the hallway, wrapping her arms around his waist.

He looked down at her in obvious surprise but returned her embrace. "What's wrong?"

She peered up at him, her face tearstained. "Sherry's been attacked."

"What?" He held his wife by the shoulders. "When? Is she okay?"

Mrs. Hamilton nodded. "Cara and Connie say she should be fine, but it looks like someone knocked her over the head on purpose. I don't understand. Why is all this happening?"

Her husband's face hardened. "This is all my fault. I've put everyone in this house at risk." He let out a breath and kissed the top of his wife's head. "I've made arrangements to deliver the ransom myself."

I noticed Reese straighten up.

Mrs. Hamilton dabbed at her eyes. "What does that mean? Will you get in trouble?"

"It doesn't matter. It's my responsibility to fix this, even if it means I go to jail."

Mrs. Hamilton began sobbing silently as her husband held her, and her mother looked on, a look of disapproval set firmly on the old woman's face.

I motioned to Richard and Reese to follow me out of the room so we could escape the awkwardness of both the private moment and the barely concealed hostility.

"Did you know anything about all this family drama?" Richard asked me once we'd reached the foyer.

"Not a clue," I said. "But at this point I couldn't care less. If the father pays the ransom, we'll get Kate back."

"You still think this is about someone getting their hands on the poison gas?" Reese asked.

"All I know is Kate is being held for a ransom which is about to be paid." I felt a flutter of excitement, but told myself not to count my chickens before they'd hatched.

"So I'm too late?"

I turned to see a dark-haired man in black cargo pants and a black henley shirt coming through the front door. For a moment I thought it was a member of Mr. Hamilton's security team.

"Isn't that . . ." Richard asked, giving the muscular man a once-over.

"Daniel Reese," I said as Mike stepped forward to give his big brother a one-armed hug. "What are you doing here?"

Reese thumped his brother on the back. "He's my backup."

Richard rubbed his head. "They're multiplying."

Aside from the touches of gray at his temples and the extra inch Daniel had on his brother, the men looked similar enough to warrant a double take. Mike's big brother was also in law enforcement, or at least he had been until he'd retired and opened his own private security firm. I'd worked with him on a previous wedding that required extra security, and he'd accompanied his brother to Bali to surprise me, but I hadn't seen him too much over the last few months. This wasn't a big deal since I was in the middle of my busy wedding season, and my cop boyfriend had been putting in extra hours so he could angle for a promotion. Most of the few hours Mike and I had managed to spend together, I hadn't wanted to share him. I wasn't even sure if Daniel knew his younger brother had floated the idea of us moving in together. Not that now was the time to bring it up.

"Hi, Annabelle," Daniel said, bending down to give me a peck on the cheek. "Hi, Richard."

"He remembered my name," Richard muttered to me as he puffed out his chest.

"How did you get in?" I asked, trying to ignore Richard preening beside me.

"I know your security guys," he said. "Some of them have worked for me."

Reese gave a brief nod. "I thought you might have some insight into them."

"I do," the older brother said. "These guys are good. If someone managed to slip by them, they'd have to be even better. Professionals."

My stomach dropped as I heard Richard's quick inhale.

"That's what I was afraid of," Reese said.

CHAPTER 19

"So what does that mean for Kate?" I asked, biting the edge of my thumbnail and feeling grateful I didn't bother with expensive manicures. "And the bride, of course."

Daniel shifted his weight from one foot to the other. "Mike gave me the bare bones information about what happened, but I don't know enough to say for sure what we're dealing with."

Richard cleared his throat. "I hate to bring this up, but how are we going to explain another tall, dark, and out-of-place guy to everyone? And before Fern even thinks about it, I do not go in for any type of ménage à trois, pretend or otherwise. Being romantically linked to one Reese brother is enough for me, thank you very much."

Daniel's eyebrows shot up so high I thought they might meld with his dark hairline.

Mike put a hand to one temple and massaged it. "It's not what it sounds like. I'll explain it to you later."

"Please do," Daniel said, the side of his mouth curling up into a half smile.

"As it stands now, the father of the bride, Mr. Stephen Hamilton, is planning to deliver the ransom by himself," Mike said. "According to the kidnappers, the bride, Veronica Hamilton, will be released, presumably with Kate, Annabelle's assistant."

"I remember Kate," Daniel said.

I was sure he did since my flirty assistant had kissed him rather enthusiastically during a moment of relief and excitement in Bali. Although they hadn't seen each other since then, and I knew Kate didn't have any serious designs on my boyfriend's older brother, I liked to think his fond memory of her would make the rescue personal for him as well.

Daniel pivoted to face his brother. "And did I hear you correctly when you told me the kidnappers aren't asking for money?"

"That's right," Reese rocked back on his heels. "They want some of the highly toxic nerve gas that Hamilton's pharmaceutical company has been developing."

Daniel frowned. "You know this is way out of our league. Even if I was on the job and you were here in an official capacity, we'd be calling in Homeland Security or the bureau."

"Yeah, I do," his brother said. "But something about this kidnapping and ransom is off. I know it seems like we're dealing with terrorists after a potentially deadly biological weapon, but my gut tells me this is less about the ransom and more about the guy who's being forced to give the ransom."

"You mean because everybody hates him?" Richard asked. "Especially his own family?"

"That and how low-tech this plan was," Reese said. "They didn't kill anyone when they extracted the two women, and the only person injured so far is a woman who was leaking family secrets to Annabelle."

"How do you explain the kidnappers getting past security?" Daniel asked.

"Until the women disappeared, the security team was solely focused on watching the dad. Either they missed it because they weren't looking for it, or the kidnapping didn't look like a kidnapping."

Daniel moved his head up and down slowly. "You mean the women left without knowing they were being kidnapped?"

"It would explain why we found no signs of a struggle and no one heard a thing."

"Outrageous!" Sidney Allen bustled into the foyer, his hands over his head. He'd clearly recovered from his earlier shock and even cleaned the grass off his face, but bright green stains still covered the front of his dress shirt and pants.

"What's going on?" I asked.

"Not only did your renegade floral designers stretch out the fabric of the two capes they took, the doge costumes are still missing as well as several of my imported Pulcinella masks." Sidney Allen took a breath and glared at me. "I cannot work under these intolerable conditions."

I put a hand on his arm, removing it just as quickly when he stared me down. "It's a stressful day for all of us."

Sidney Allen paced a small circle on the marble floor. "How can guests be welcomed by an authentic Venetian doge and his retinue if I don't have the costumes I had made for the doge and his wife?" He stopped and gave us all hard looks. "What kind of person would steal costumes?"

Richard sniffed and picked a piece of imaginary lint off his beige suit jacket. "Don't look at me, little man. Wild horses couldn't get me into embroidered satin on a summer day like today."

"Well, I'm going to question every single person here until I track down the culprit." Sidney Allen hooked his thumbs through the belt loops of his pants and jerked them up. "Starting with those two thugs you call florists."

"Good luck with that," I said to his back as he stomped out of the foyer in the direction of the kitchen.

"I thought we were dealing with an abduction, not costume theft," Daniel said.

"That was Sidney Allen," I explained. "He's putting together all the performers and entertainment for today's wedding. Since we're trying to recreate Carnival in Venice, it's a pretty tall order. It seems someone made off with a couple of his costumes."

"You know," Reese said. "I may talk to that little fellow just to rule out the possibility that his missing costumes aren't connected to the abduction."

"You aren't suggesting someone is randomly snatching things from the wedding, are you?" Richard asked. "First the bride and a wedding planner, next some costumes."

Reese cocked an eyebrow at him. "Not exactly, but I've found that coincidences rarely are just that."

"And I'm assuming the thug florists are your friends Buster and Mack?" Daniel asked.

"Did someone say our names?" Mack called out as he ambled into the foyer from the hallway with Buster right behind him. Both men looked startled and pleased when they spotted Daniel. "It's a Bali reunion!"

"Except for Kate," I said, instantly regretting my words as their faces fell.

Mack took Reese's hand while looking at me. "We have faith the detective will get her back."

"And the bride," I reminded them, knowing Veronica hadn't been their easiest or favorite client.

"Of course," Buster said. "Her too."

"We've got the entire North American network of the Road Riders for Jesus on the case," Mack said, taking Daniel's hand as well. "And then you show up."

Buster lifted his eyes to the ceiling. "It goes to show you the power of prayer."

"Didn't Loverboy call him?" Richard whispered to me.

"Pet names already?" I asked and watched patches of red appear on Richard's cheeks.

"So who are we going to say he is?" Reese asked, looking at his brother dressed in black. "At least he's dressed like half the people here setting up the wedding."

"We can say he's on our crew," Mack said. "We always need buff guys to help us with the heavy lifting."

"So I'm pretending to be a florist?" Daniel asked.

"When it's this fancy, it's a design installation," Buster said. "We've got a custom stage and dance floor, not to mention the backdrop behind the band and all the hanging chandeliers."

His brother leaned closer to him. "Consider yourself lucky. I'm going incognito as a sommelier romantically involved with my boss."

Richard sniffed and folded his arms across his chest. "You should be so lucky."

The opera singer who had been practicing earlier strode through the foyer, singing scales with one arm outstretched as he walked. A pair of purple-and-green-striped stilts appeared, being carried horizontally by a man in a matching costume with puffy pantaloons and black tights. The man crossed the foyer and entered the far hallway, the end of the stilts trailing after him.

"This is a wedding, right?" Daniel asked.

"A slightly crazy one, but yes," Mack said.

"Speaking of crazy, you didn't run into Sidney Allen on your way here, did you?" I asked Buster and Mack.

"The little fellow who's losing his mind over his costumes?" Buster asked. "We apologized for borrowing the capes, but he's insisting we stretched them out."

Mack rolled his eyes. "How do you stretch out a cape, I ask you?"

"I don't know, but I hope he finds the doge costumes fast. He's right when he says we can't exactly have an authentic doge and his entourage greeting the guests without the doge." I wondered if there was any truth to Reese's concerns the missing costumes were connected to the missing bride and Kate, but I couldn't see how.

"First things first." Richard held up a finger. "If we don't have a bride, we don't have a wedding."

"We don't have to worry about that anymore," Fern said from the doorway leading into the kitchen.

"What do you mean?" I asked, turning to face my friend as he leaned against the doorjamb. "Is the mother of the bride finally giving up the idea of saving this wedding?"

Fern shook his head. "Mr. Hamilton left to make the ransom drop a few minutes ago. If all goes according to plan, Kate and Veronica will be back here soon."

I exchanged a look with Reese, and I knew we were thinking the same thing. What happened if everything didn't go according to plan?

CHAPTER 20

"*H*ow long has it been since Mr. Hamilton left?" I asked Fern as Daniel, Mike, and I traipsed upstairs behind him.

"Not long." Fern glanced over his shoulder when he reached the top of the curving staircase. "So there's no need to watch the clock yet."

Easier said than done, I thought. I snuck a peek at my phone. It was already five o'clock. We were getting closer and closer to the ceremony time, and we still were missing a bride. I told myself not to think about the wedding, but that only made me focus on the ransom drop. I wasn't sure what to think about the bride's father taking off to pay the ransom since Mike seemed convinced that the poison gas wasn't the key element of the kidnapping. If he was right, would giving the kidnappers what they claimed to want even matter?

"Anyway, if the bride will be back soon, I need to wrangle her hussies into shape." Fern tucked a loose strand back into his high man bun.

"Hussies?" Daniel said from behind me.

"That's what he calls all bridesmaids," I explained, resting one hand on the gleaming wooden bannister overlooking the spacious foyer. "Unless he's calling them tramps or floozies."

Fern winked at Daniel. "I tell them it's a term of affection."

"Is it?" Mike asked, resting one hand on the small of my back.

Fern smiled and bobbed his head as he headed down the hallway toward the sound of female voices. "What they don't know . . ."

"Are we going to hang out with the bridesmaids?" Mike asked. "I could barely pull off being a fake sommelier. There's no way I can make a convincing hairstylist."

I laughed. "I thought we'd show your brother the bride's room since it's the last place she and Kate were seen. And it keeps both of you tucked away."

I also needed to get away from the chaos of the wedding setup and the Hamiltons for a few minutes. Between the drama of the wedding and the drama of the bride's family, not to mention that of my own crew, I was in serious need of some calm within the storm.

I glanced at the framed family portraits hanging on the wall as I followed Fern down the hallway, each of them a picture-perfect vignette of the Hamiltons smiling widely. The only noticeable change in each photo was the gradual aging of the three children and the different outfits—winter sweaters outside in the woods in one, jeans and white T-shirts on the beach in another, blazers and dresses by the fireplace in a third. Mr. and Mrs. Hamilton looked remarkably similar from image to image, a testament to the kind of skin care and amount of Botox money could buy.

When we reached Veronica's bedroom, I waved the two Reese brothers inside. "Why don't you two take a look around while I poke my head in the bridesmaids' room for a second?"

Fern stopped further down the hall to wait for me. "Venturing into the belly of the beast?"

"They can't be that bad," I said. Since the wedding had such intensive setup, I'd spent less time than usual with the bridesmaids, but I felt confident this group couldn't be any more challenging than some of my past ones.

"None of them are cold-blooded killers," Fern said, and I knew he was referencing one of our past weddings and the unfortunate turn of events regarding one member of the bridal party. "At least that we know of."

"I'm going to take that as a positive," I said.

"Take the wins where you can get them, sweetie."

Fern pushed open the door to the room where the bridesmaids were getting ready, and the volume of giggling and chatter increased dramatically. The expansive bedroom I assumed was Val's had the same layout as the bride's room with a small sitting nook, and en suite bathroom, and windows overlooking the back of the house. But where Veronica's room was decorated in neutrals, this room was bathed in shades of purple. From the lavender duvet cover to the plum throw pillows to the violet curtains, it was tone on tone with the ivory carpet as the only thing not purple.

"Wow," I said.

"It's like Barney threw up in here, isn't it?" Fern muttered to me before parading into the room and starting to fuss over the girls.

I noticed the long-haired photographer standing in the corner snapping the occasional getting-ready photo and felt glad she didn't have a clue the group photos may be taking place sans bride.

"There you are," one of the bridesmaids said, her words slurring as she lay sprawled across the bed in a shimmery floral robe.

The blonde next to her rolled onto her stomach and pushed herself onto her elbows. "We're dying of boredom up here."

For women whose close friend had been kidnapped, they didn't seem too broken up. I noticed the empty champagne bottles strewn across the nightstand and vanity, along with at least a dozen empty crystal flutes. Whatever food had been here was long gone.

"Can I bring you any snacks?" I asked, while Fern plopped a girl down onto his stool by the window and began unspooling her curlers.

"You're one of the wedding planners, right?" A tall woman whose floral robe barely reached mid thigh came out of the bathroom. "The other one checked on us earlier."

"Kate?" I said.

"Sounds right," the woman said. "So when do we need to get into our dresses?"

I looked at the row of plastic dry cleaning bags hanging from the top of the bathroom door. I knew they held the long, crimson one-shoulder bridesmaids' dresses with thin ribbon belts that would be worn once and never again.

"Soon," I said, attempting to sound more confident than I felt.

The room smelled of hairspray and stale champagne, and as I looked at the Louis Vuitton duffel bags and Longchamp totes with their contents spilling out onto the floor, I wondered who was going to clean up the mess. Even though I'd ended up playing the maid at one too many weddings to count, I had no intention of closing out this wedding day like that.

"I can't believe Veronica isn't back yet." The blond bridesmaid on the bed swung her legs over the side.

"It's not like she snuck out for a smoke." The other woman on the bed punched her lightly on the arm. "She's been kidnapped, remember?"

"I'd kill for a smoke," a brunette with a tattoo on her ankle said. "I don't suppose we can do that inside, can we?"

Another bridesmaid wrinkled her nose. "You and your smoking. When are you going to quit?"

"Hey, I'm not the only one." The brunette ran a hand through her bushy hair, and something about her sparked a flicker of recognition. Had this girl been a bridesmaid in another of our weddings? The DC area was small enough that we got client overlap, especially since most of our business came from word-of-mouth referrals.

The blonde shook her head. "It doesn't seem real. Why would anyone want to take Veronica?"

"Forget that," the tall bridesmaid said. "Why would anyone want to keep her?"

"You're horrible," the bridesmaid on Fern's stool said, although she laughed as she said it.

"What? I'm only saying she isn't the most low-maintenance girl in the world." The tall woman crossed to the window and pulled the curtain back so she could look outside. "I'm surprised the kidnappers didn't drive her back within half an hour and drop her off outside the gate."

All the girls laughed, and Fern raised his eyebrows at me over the bridesmaid's head as he ran both his hands through her hair to fluff it up. I wasn't sure if I should add all eight bridesmaids to my mental list of potential suspects, or chalk it up to bitchy brides having bitchy friends.

I caught Fern's eye and pointed to the door. "I'm going to go check on . . ."

"Go." He waved a hand at me while he used the other to deposit a cloud of hairspray over the bridesmaid in his chair. "I've got this covered."

I left the room, glad to escape the chatter and hairspray, and returned to the bride's room where Daniel and Mike both stood at the window. "Anything new?"

Mike turned, smiling when he saw me. "Nothing. Daniel agrees with what we thought."

"No struggle of any kind." Daniel walked to the middle of the room and opened his arms wide. "It's like they vanished."

"Except for the phones and gummy bear," I said.

"If Kate was leaving you a trail of candy, she didn't leave a long one," Daniel said.

Mike came over and took my fingers. "My brother thinks the gummy bear was accidentally dropped."

"Oh." I felt a bit of my hope evaporate. "I guess that makes more sense."

"There you all are," Richard said, throwing his hands in the air. "I've been looking everywhere."

"What's wrong?" I asked.

"You mean aside from the obvious?" Richard's eyes flitted to my fingers entwined with Reese's and visibly twitched. "Nothing. I can't stand the waiting."

"What are you all doing in here?" the bride's younger sister asked from the door.

I dropped Reese's hand and hoped she hadn't noticed since he was supposed to be involved with Richard, not me. I hadn't heard her coming down the hall, but the carpet was pretty plush and her feet were bare. Her cousin, Cara, stood behind her.

"Cleaning up some of the empties." I picked up a champagne bottle. "So your sister comes back to a clean room."

"It really is a disaster," Richard said as if noticing his surroundings for the first time. He unfurled a handkerchief from his inside jacket pocket and headed for the cluttered vanity table.

Val didn't look convinced, but Cara smiled.

"How's Sherry?" I asked the bride's cousin.

"Good. She's still out of it but her vitals are fine, and there doesn't seem to be much swelling or bleeding."

"Any chance she can tell us who attacked her?" Daniel asked.

Cara sized him up as she stepped into the room. "And who might you be?"

"I'm with the florist," he said after a beat, motioning to the box of bouquets at the end of the bed. "I'm checking on the flowers up here before finishing the installation behind the stage."

I tried not to look as impressed as I felt by Daniel's use of designer lingo.

"Sounds fancy. I'm sure my aunt and uncle spared no expense for this wedding," Cara said, not questioning Daniel's cover story. "And to answer your question, I doubt she'll be talking anytime soon. My mother is with her now, and I just told her daughter so she can go be with her. If Sherry comes to, they can let us know."

So much for our one eyewitness. "Her daughter is here? How did she get past security?" How incompetent was this security team?

"She's a bridesmaid," Cara said.

The girl with brown hair and the tattoo. I knew I'd recognized her from somewhere. I just hadn't made the connection to the photo I'd seen in Sherry's office.

"Stephanie practically grew up here," Val said. "She's like family. Better than family, actually, because she's not a self-absorbed snob like my sister."

"So you're not eager to have your sister back?" Daniel asked.

Val slanted her eyes at him. "If you're trying to suggest I'm happy she was kidnapped, you're wrong. But I'm not holding my breath she'll be back. You shouldn't either."

"What do you mean?" Richard asked, his handkerchief stopping in mid flutter over the vanity.

"Your father has already gone to pay the ransom," I said, thinking she might not have heard.

"I know." Val lifted one shoulder. "My father talks a good game but doesn't always do what he says he's going to."

I felt my mouth go dry. "You think he lied to your mother about paying the ransom?"

"It wouldn't be the first time he lied to her."

"Come on, Val," Cara said, laughing uncomfortably. "I'm sure these people don't want to hear all the family's dirty laundry."

"It's not like it's your dirty laundry." There was an edge to Val's voice. "It's not your dad who's banged every secretary he's ever had."

Cara flinched at the sharp reply.

"All of them?" Richard asked, giving me a look of incredulity and dropping his voice. "Well, someone's certainly been a busy little boy."

"He's not picky," Val said. "And if he's lied about working late for the past twenty-five years, who knows what else he's lied about?"

She made a good point. Mr. Hamilton had basically admitted to Reese and Richard that he'd gotten the DOD contract through underhanded means.

"Having an affair is different than leaving your sister in the hands of kidnappers," I said. "Do you really think he wouldn't want to save Veronica?"

"Over his own skin?" Val shrugged. "Who knows? If it was me in Veronica's place, I'd be hoping for a rescue instead of counting on dear old dad. But she's always been his favorite child, so who knows?"

None of this made me feel any better about our chances of getting Kate back. I pulled my phone out of my dress pocket and looked at the time. Reese stepped closer to me and touched a finger to the hand by my side, and I knew that was his way of telling me not to worry.

"Hello, handsome," Richard said.

For a moment I thought he meant Mike. Before I could compliment him for embracing his role, I noticed his line of sight out the window to the pool and yard. I joined him at the window.

"That guy looks way too fresh to be involved in the wedding setup." Richard eyed the sandy-haired man in khakis and a crisp poppy-colored button-down shirt standing below us on the pool deck and talking on his cell phone. "And I know he isn't one of mine."

"He's not wearing a costume or a mask, so I doubt he's one of Sidney Allen's," I said, watching the man look up at the house and wave.

"He's wearing designer," Richard said. "Imported. Custom-made Italian, if I'm not mistaken."

I squinted at the man. I could barely make out more than the color of his clothing. "How can you tell from all the way up here?"

Richard winked at me. "It's a gift, darling."

Daniel and his brother crossed to the window.

"So if he's not involved with the wedding, why is he loitering outside the house?" Daniel asked.

"Him?" Val peered around my shoulder and gave a dismissive laugh. "That's the husband of my mother's best friend and my father's most bitter rival."

I tightened my grip on Mike's hand. Tarek Nammour was here?

"It's also the man my mother has been sleeping with," Val called back as she walked out of the room.

135

"*H*old on a second." I ran out of the bedroom after Val and caught her by the arm. "You know your mom's been having an affair?"

She looked down at my hand and gave me an impatient look until I removed it. "There are a lot of secrets in this family that aren't quite secret."

Val continued her dramatic exit down the hall followed by her cousin, who cast an apologetic look over her shoulder.

"I'm taking it there are a lot of closets filled with skeletons around here," Daniel said when he, Richard, and Reese joined me outside the bedroom.

"Let's hope not literally," I said. With my track record for stumbling onto dead bodies, an actual skeleton falling out of a closet wasn't so farfetched. I headed toward the stairs. "We should go talk to this Tarek guy."

"Probably," Reese said. "But what's our pretense? I'm supposed to be a wine guy, and Daniel is a florist."

"He doesn't know that." I lowered my voice. "Tell him you're with the security team, and you need to ask him some questions in light of what's happened. With the way you two look, he won't doubt you for a second."

"What about me?" Richard asked. "Are you saying I wouldn't be convincing as a security officer?"

I paused at the top of the curving staircase, thinking how best to phrase my next sentence so I wouldn't be on Richard's bad side for the next month.

"I think you'd be convincing," Reese said before I could speak. "You should come with us."

"It's nice to know some people notice my versatility." Richard gave Reese a brief smile and me a dirty look as he started down the stairs. "I'm not just a pretty face, you know, Annabelle."

I didn't know whether to hug Mike for trying to include Richard or punch him for making me look like the bad guy in comparison.

When we'd reached the foyer, I pointed to the hall leading to the right. "Why don't you three wait in Mr. Hamilton's study? Since the bride's father is off paying the ransom, it should be empty. I'll bring Tarek to you so no one will see you with him and wonder what you're all doing."

"And you?" Reese asked. "What if someone sees you escorting him inside?"

"I'm the wedding planner," I said. "I can tell anyone what to do and no one will think twice about it."

The three men walked in one direction and I went in the other, passing through the casual dining room and kitchen and stepping out the French doors and onto the terrace. The man turned when he heard me behind him, and I was struck by how attractive he was up close.

His sandy hair was wavy and a little long, curling up around the nape of his neck, and his was the kind of tan you got from being outside and not from a bronzer or a bottle. His eyes were a warm brown, and the skin around them crinkled when he smiled at me. I could see why Mrs. Hamilton would be attracted to him.

"Maybe you can help me," he said, clicking his phone off. "I'm here to see Deborah."

"Mrs. Hamilton?" I beckoned for him to come with me. "I'll take you to her."

I retraced my steps back through the house with Tarek Nammour behind me and directed him to the heavy wooden doors leading to Mr. Hamilton's study. He eyed them and hesitated.

"I need you to wait here while I get her."

He pushed open the doors and slipped inside where I knew Daniel, Mike, and Richard would be waiting. I caught the door before it closed and pushed it open so I could listen at the crack.

"Who are you all?" Mr. Nammour asked.

"We're with Mr. Hamilton's security team, and we have a few questions for you," Daniel said. "Why don't you have a seat?"

I heard the sound of creaking leather and assumed Tarek sat down on one of the brown leather sofas. "I know what happened to Veronica. My wife and Deborah Hamilton are best friends, so she called after it happened."

"And that was the first you were aware of the kidnapping and ransom?" Mike asked.

"Of course. You don't think I'm somehow connected to this because Stephen and I are professional rivals, do you?"

"Don't try to play the unsuspecting innocent with us, buster," Richard said, sounding less like a security officer than anyone I'd ever heard. "Just because you're insanely good-looking and have the body of a Greek god doesn't mean you'll get away with it."

I put my head in my hands. At least Richard's involvement hadn't been my idea. My boyfriend had no one to blame but himself for this one.

"What my associate means is we aren't accusing you of anything, sir." Daniel's voice sounded firm. "We are, however, interested in your timeline for today."

"Timeline? You mean what I've been doing?" The man took a breath. "I played some golf this morning, then went home. I've been home with my wife while she got ready for the wedding until I came over here. My golf buddies can back me up, as can my wife."

"Would you be surprised to know Mr. Hamilton named you as the person he says has the most to gain from this kidnapping and ransom request?" Mike asked.

"What? That's absurd."

"Not as absurd as you might like it to be," Richard said.

I wondered if I should run in the room and tackle him before he could speak again.

"What?" Tarek sounded confused, not that I blamed him.

"Who's in my husband's study?" Mrs. Hamilton asked as she came down the stairs still in her robe, but with her hair in loose curls around her shoulders.

"Exactly what I was wondering, Mrs. Hamilton," I said, raising my voice to a near shout. "Who's in there?"

She pushed past me into the room, spotted Tarek Nammour, and ran toward him. He stood up and took her in his arms as she dissolved into tears.

"It's going to be fine, Deborah," Tarek said as he stroked her hair. "All of this is going to work out."

She sobbed harder.

Richard, Daniel, and Mike drifted toward the door as I backed further into the hallway, bumping into someone and turning around to see the bride's father glowering over me at his wife.

"In my own house?" Mr. Hamilton bellowed, pushing me to one side as he charged into the room.

His wife stepped out of Tarek's embrace, spinning to meet her husband with equal fire. "Now I can't even be consoled by a friend?"

"Is that what we're calling it now?" Mr. Hamilton's laugh was rough. "Consoling?"

Richard hurried out of the room and clutched my arm. "Do you think we have time to pop some popcorn?"

"This is rich," Mrs. Hamilton threw back her head. "Are you really getting angry at me for being unfaithful?"

"I don't care who you sleep with, dear," her husband spat out his words, "as long as it's not him."

Tarek took a step toward his rival. "Don't you talk to her like that."

"Do you think this is going to get ugly?" I said to Richard. "Should we call the police?"

Richard held up two fingers. "One, it's already ugly. And two?" He pointed to Daniel and Mike as they backed toward us, their eyes on the exploding love triangle. "We have our own cops."

"I can't believe this." Mr. Hamilton jabbed a finger in his wife's direction. "I'm off paying the ransom to save our daughter, and you're carrying on behind my back."

"You're the reason Veronica was kidnapped in the first place," Mrs. Hamilton screamed. "All of this is your fault."

"And I suppose it's my fault you're sleeping with your best friend's husband?" Mr. Hamilton matched his wife's volume, and I backed further away.

Mrs. Hamilton narrowed her eyes until they were slits. "At least I didn't sleep with the help."

Her husband's mouth dropped open, as Tarek stared back and forth between the pair. I suspected this was more than he'd bargained for when he'd started the affair or decided to pop over to the house.

Richard's grip on my arm tightened. "I've seen telenovelas with less drama than this."

I rubbed my forehead. "If someone turns out to have an evil twin, I'm out of here."

CHAPTER 22

"**W**ell, that was awkward," Richard said as we regrouped with Daniel and Mike in the foyer.

We could still hear raised voices as the Hamiltons argued, but standing in the doorway and watching them rip into each other had seemed voyeuristic, so I'd hustled everyone out and closed the study doors to muffle the sounds. Even now, my first instinct was to protect my client and keep the wedding day humming along.

"You know who would be in her element?" I asked no one in particular.

"Kate," Richard said, not meeting my eyes.

I cleared my throat to keep my voice from cracking. "Although with her Jedi skills when it comes to romantic entanglements, I'm surprised she didn't call some of this earlier. She can usually tell if people are having an affair or are in love at fifty paces."

"Did she spend much time with the Hamiltons together?" Richard asked.

"You're right. She didn't." I felt my eyes water as I thought fondly of Kate and how she'd predicted my relationship with Reese before I was even sure he liked me. I forced myself to think positively. "Good thing she'll be back soon, and I can fill her in on all the drama she's missed."

Richard twisted to face Mike. "How long until we should expect Veronica and Kate to be let go?"

Reese exchanged a look with his brother before answering. "If the kidnappers got what they wanted, it shouldn't be long."

"Good." Richard nodded brusquely. "I, for one, have a five-course Venetian dinner to pull off, and these shenanigans have been more than a little distracting."

I pulled the wedding day schedule out of my dress pocket and flipped through the crinkled pages. "We shouldn't be too far behind, and it's not like we stopped setup. I'm sure once the bride is back, we can make up time somewhere. Maybe we cut the cocktail hour to forty-five minutes instead of an hour?"

Richard sucked in air. "You want to cut my cocktail hour? After all the time I spent coming up with the specialty cocktails and customizing the hors d'oeuvres?"

"How do you customize an hors d'oeuvre?" Reese asked me out of the side of his mouth.

"For one thing, they aren't technically called hors d'oeuvres." Richard put his hands on his hips. "The Venetians call their small bites cicchetti. I'm serving one dish I found in a Venetian cookbook from the 1300s, and I'm pairing it with the perfect cocktail: a Campari spritzer made with Prosecco."

"Richard likes to be historically accurate with his cuisine," I explained.

"My cicchetti can't be rushed, Annabelle," Richard said. "Can you take time from someplace else? What about the ceremony? Those things can really drag on."

I leveled my eyes at him. "You want me to cut out the part where the couple legally gets married? The entire point of the day?"

"Not cut it out, darling. Just trim the fat." He made cutting motions with two fingers. "Snip, snip."

"I'll see what I can do," I said, knowing I had zero intention of shortening the ceremony. Officiants were rarely receptive to suggestions they cut out scripture readings in favor of custom cocktails.

Daniel turned to his brother. "I'd like to check on the other victim. Maybe she's regained consciousness enough to give us some information. Even if Kate and your bride come back, we still have to deal with the attempted murder."

Since Sherry had survived, it was easy for me to forget that killing her had most likely been the aim of the attack. This was no small matter since no one had left the property, which meant we still had a violent criminal running loose.

"Do you want to come with us?" Reese asked, resting a hand lightly on my back.

I took out my phone and glanced at the time, feeling a nervous flutter that we were just over an hour away from when guests might start arriving. "I'd better go with Richard and check the reception and dinner setup. If the bride reappears soon, everything will move pretty fast, and we need to be ready."

He leaned down and brushed his lips to my cheek in a quick kiss. "Okay, but don't go anywhere alone. We've already had two people kidnapped and one attacked. I don't want anything to happen to you."

Richard linked his arm through mine. "Don't worry, Detective. I'll keep an eye on her."

I wasn't sure if this was truly comforting to him, but Reese patted Richard on the shoulder and thanked him.

"So," I said as Richard led me through the casual dining room and kitchen, "you and Reese seem to be making friends."

Richard gave me a side-eye glance. "I wouldn't go that far, but he has shown an appreciation for my talents lately. Something certain people could learn from."

I ignored the not-so-subtle dig.

Richard opened the French doors leading outside, and I shielded my eyes as we stepped onto the back terrace leading to the pool deck. The sun sat lower in the sky but still burned brightly, warming my skin and making me miss the air conditioning of the house almost instantly. I enjoyed the fact that the June sun didn't set until after eight o'clock in the evening, but that also meant more hours of heat. I took a breath, inhaling both humidity and smoke in equal measure. I put a hand over my nose and coughed.

"Sorry." Aunt Connie stood a few feet away and waved a hand to dissipate the cloud of cigarette smoke surrounding her. "I know it's a bad habit. My daughter gives me all kinds of grief about it. Says I should know better, especially since I'm a nurse."

"It's okay," I said, stifling another urge to cough. "I know it's been a rough day."

The woman dropped her cigarette and ground it under her foot into one of the beige paving stones. "I keep saying I'm going to quit, then the first time something stresses me out, I run right back."

I tried not to focus on the cigarette butt I would now need to come back out and clean off the terrace before guests arrived. "I get it."

"Any word?" Aunt Connie asked, a furrow forming between her eyes.

"Well, Mr. Hamilton delivered the ransom, so we're hoping Veronica and my assistant will be released soon."

"Good. He's put my sister through plenty, so this is the least he could do for her and his daughter."

I didn't know what to say, so I smiled. Richard's phone trilled and he pulled it out of his jacket pocket, sighing when he saw the name on the screen.

"What on earth could it be this time, Leatrice?" He paused to listen. "Hermes's bedtime is whenever he falls asleep. He's a dog."

Aunt Connie looked a little confused as she walked past us into the house.

"No, I don't think he'll be permanently scarred if he watches *Old Yeller*. You aren't taking him to a movie theatre, are you?"

I took a few steps closer to the pool, which was now penguin-free, and wondered where the little animals were hanging out. My eyes drifted to the pool house at the far end of the pool, which looked like a Tuscan villa that had been shrunk. This was where we had all of the performers staged, along with their food, so it made sense the penguins were hiding out in there, although I doubted they ate luncheon meat or snickerdoodles.

My own stomach growled as I thought about food, and I realized it had been hours since I'd eaten a bite. This happened to me at almost every wedding, because I got too busy to think about food until I was light-headed. My stomach was making noises loud enough to be heard by Richard.

"Good heavens," he said, holding his hand over his phone. "Was that you?"

Before I could defend myself, I caught a glimpse of one of the waiters walking through the reception tent. I recognized the gait as being distinctively female, although the waiter had boy-cut blond hair. This in and of itself wasn't something notable, but something in the stride made me squint my eyes to get a better look.

The waiter looked up and locked eyes with me, and I gasped. The blonde in the bistro apron ran from the large dinner tent into the draped one next to it, disappearing behind a wall of fabric.

I rushed over to Richard and shook his arm. "I just saw Tina Pink dressed up like one of your waiters."

Richard lowered the phone from his ear. "What? That's impossible. What would that disgraced wedding planner be doing here?"

"Revenge," I said, feeling my heart pound. "What if this entire kidnapping doesn't have anything to do with the Hamiltons, but is really an elaborate plot to get back at us? What if Tina Pink is the one holding Kate hostage?"

CHAPTER 23

"Come on." I pulled Richard with me as I ran around the side of the pool toward the two reception tents. "We need to see if I'm right and that really was Tina Pink or if I'm losing my mind."

"Can't both of those be true?"

I led the way through the open sides of the dinner tent, weaving my way between the ornately decorated tables topped with towering floral and feather arrangements. The chandeliers were illuminated, and the lighting team had focused the pin spots so light now sparkled off the gilded and jeweled masks sitting on every plate.

"Don't bump the tables," Richard yelled from behind me as I sucked in my stomach and squeezed between the gold ladder-backed chairs crowned with organza-beaded chair caps.

I made it through the gauntlet of tables and chairs and reached the draped entrance to the cocktail tent, pulling back the heavy crimson fabric and stepping into the second, smaller tent. I paused inside and let my eyes adjust to the lower lighting for a moment.

While the dinner tent was bathed in light and filled with crystal, white feathers, and glimmering gold, Buster and Mack had designed the cocktail tent to reflect the mysterious and sultry side of Carnival.

Surrounded by crimson fabric walls, the space had a black-and-white checkerboard floor with gold scroll-patterned light reflected onto both it and the high-peaked ceiling. A mirrored bar stretched across the far end of the tent, and tall cocktail tables draped in black-sequined linens were scattered throughout.

I felt the air conditioning pumping into the tent from two units in the back, and the beads of sweat that had gathered at the nape of my neck immediately cooled. Guests would welcome this cool space after the ceremony in the open tent with only fans to move the air.

Richard opened the flaps of his jacket. "This is divine. Remind me why we didn't air condition all the tents?"

"Because Mrs. Hamilton didn't want to lose the view of her estate. If we put in AC, you know we have to put up fabric walls to keep the cool air inside." My eyes scanned the tent for people and any trace of the person I believed to be Tina Pink. A pair of bartenders were stocking the bar, and a few waiters placed beaded votive candles on the tables, but none of them were the blond woman I'd recognized.

"I'm willing to make the sacrifice," Richard said.

I threw my arms in the air. "Where did she go?"

"Look." Richard pointed to a section of the fabric tent walls in the back, a sliver of sunlight entering the dimly lit space as the drape was pulled open and fell back again.

I noticed a flash of blond hair ducking between the folds of crimson fabric and headed toward it, instinctively hopping out of my shoes before I scuffed the polished black-and-white squares of the dance floor. "That's her."

Richard ran around the dance floor since he couldn't easily slip out of his lace-up oxfords, but I made it to the back of the tent first and burst through the back of it, looking right and left for Tina Pink. There was no sign of her.

"Do you see her?" Richard asked, pawing at the voluminous fabric as he fought his way out of the tent.

"She's gone," I said, looking between the back of the house and the door that led to the garage-turned-catering-kitchen. "And I don't know which way she went."

Richard kicked the last bit of fabric from around his ankle. "Are you sure it was Tina Pink?"

"Pretty sure." I thought back to the moment I'd locked eyes with her and had seen the familiar flash of anger. "If it wasn't her, why did she take off running?"

"Maybe because a deranged wedding planner and her incredibly stylish friend were chasing her?" Richard suggested.

"You didn't see the way she looked at me." I began trudging around the tent to the house, still holding my black flats dangling by two fingers. "If that wasn't Tina Pink, then one of your waiters has serious anger management issues."

"You can't honestly believe I would hire Tina Pink as a waiter," Richard said, matching my steps. "I do remember what she looks like you know."

I paused at the French doors leading inside the house. "First off, she cut her long hair, so now she looks like a boy. And secondly, you might not have hired her. She may be here pretending to be a waiter. It wouldn't be difficult to show up in black pants and a white shirt, swipe a bistro apron, and wander around like you know what you're doing. No one would think twice about it."

Richard opened the door for me and held it while I stepped inside. "I like to think there's more to being a waiter with Richard Gerard Catering than that, Annabelle. You know I require my staff to have a thorough knowledge of both Russian and French service."

"I doubt she was going to grab a tray and serve filet mignon," I said. "The only reason Tina Pink would be here is because she's involved in the kidnapping."

"Tina Pink?" Mack said from where he stood at the kitchen sink filling a pair of plastic spray bottles. "Are you saying she's here?"

Aside from Mack, the kitchen was empty, but the air held the scent of coffee, and I saw that the stack of muffins in the middle of the oval table had dwindled in size. I wondered if my crew was stress eating or if the family had started to eat their feelings.

"Annabelle is convinced she saw her disguised as one of my waiters," Richard said. "We chased after her but didn't catch her, and I never got a good look."

Mack gaped at me, his jaw slack as water overflowed the spray bottles and cascaded onto his hands. "If she's here then that means . .
."

"This entire mess may not be about the Hamiltons at all, and it may be completely unrelated to any sort of terrorism." I lowered my voice. "It could be Tina Pink getting revenge on Wedding Belles."

Mack turned off the water and shook the water droplets off his beefy hands. "If it's revenge she's after, she could just as easily be after Buster and me. After all, we were partly responsible for bringing her husband to justice."

"I think if it comes to kidnapping, Kate is an easier target than the two of you," I said.

Richard leaned against the marble countertop. "Let's say Tina Pink did kidnap Kate and the bride. Why is she still running around here?"

"Maybe part of the fun is seeing us worry?" I said, although I didn't really believe it.

"Do you really think a former wedding planner could do this?" Mack asked. "This is a pretty serious crime."

"And was she a great planner in the first place?" Richard drummed his fingers on the white-and-gray marble. "This plan took some serious coordination. I honestly didn't think that bimbo had it in her."

"Which bimbo?" Fern asked, coming into the kitchen with an empty champagne bottle in each hand. "Kim, Kylie, Kendall?"

"Tina," I said, opening the under cabinet recycling bin for Fern.

Fern dropped the bottles and tilted his head at me. "Which show is she on?"

"She's not," I said. "We're talking about Tina Pink."

"That awful wedding planner with the even more awful husband?" Fern hiccupped. "I still have nightmares about him coming after me."

"Annabelle thinks she saw Tina here," Mack said.

"What?" Fern looked wildly around. "What would she be doing here? You don't think she's come to finish off the job, do you?"

"If it was, in fact, Tina I saw with her hair cut like a man and dressed up like a waiter," I said, "I think she may be involved in the kidnapping."

Fern staggered over to one of the chairs and collapsed into it. "Poor Kate."

"You weren't worried about her before?" I asked.

"Of course I was." Fern wrung his hands in his lap. "But it's one thing to be taken by terrorists and quite another to be kidnapped by an insane wedding planner."

"We don't know she's insane," Richard said. "Having bad taste doesn't mean she's certifiable, although you wouldn't get any arguments from me if that became the new litmus test."

"You said she cut off her long, blond hair and now has a man's haircut?" Fern asked.

"If it was her, then yes," I told him. "And not a cute pixie cut, either. It looked like she'd gone to a military barber."

"I rest my case." Fern raised and lowered his eyebrows slowly. "In-sane."

"If she is involved, what can we do?" Mack asked, holding his two spray bottles at his waist like guns.

"First we have to find her and make sure it's actually Tina Pink," I said. "There's a possibility I'm wrong."

"Wrong about what?" Daniel asked as he and his brother came into the room.

"Annabelle thinks she spotted Tina Pink posing as a waiter," Mack explained.

Daniel's face remained blank, but recognition crossed Mike's face. "The one with the husband and the big pool brouhaha?" he asked. "Isn't she a wedding planner too?"

"*Was* a wedding planner," Richard corrected him. "Past tense. I haven't heard a peep about her since that day, not that she ever had much business in the first place. I honestly don't know how all these new planners stay in business. Plan your own wedding, throw out a shingle, take a bunch of photos of pretty tabletops and selfies drinking coffee and, poof, you're an Instagram star with no income."

We all stared at Richard.

"Sorry. Sometimes I need to vent." He gave a flourish of his hand. "Carry on."

"So this former colleague is now here working as a waiter?" Daniel asked.

Richard put a palm to his chest. "*I* didn't hire her. I have exceedingly high standards for my service staff. I highly doubt she'd make the cut."

Reese walked over and put a hand on my waist. "So what are you thinking?"

I closed my eyes for a moment to keep from tearing up. When I opened them, I gazed up at him, meeting his hazel eyes. "I think this kidnapping may have nothing to do with the DOD or the ransom or the Hamiltons. It might be all about Tina Pink getting revenge on us for ruining her life."

"We don't know her life was ruined," Fern said. "We don't even know for sure her hair is ruined."

"Yes we do." The voice from the doorway was accompanied by a small yip.

Richard's head snapped around. "Leatrice! Hermes! What are the two of you doing here?"

It took me a moment to realize my nutty neighbor was wearing Richard's tiny Yorkie in a front-facing baby carrier, the dog's brown-and-black head peeking out over the top, and his little legs extending in front of him.

"I heard you yelling about Tina Pink when I was on the phone with Richard, and then I heard you say Kate had been kidnapped." Leatrice shook her head, but her jet-black Mary Tyler Moore flip did not budge. "We were already in my car on the way to the movies, and I knew you needed my help, so Hermes and I rushed over."

I didn't bother to ask how she found us since Leatrice considered herself to be an amateur spy and kept me under constant surveillance. It would not surprise me if she had a tracker on my car or phone or both. "How did you get past the guards?"

"They asked if I was performing the ceremony and I said yes." She rubbed her hands together. "Do you need me to perform the ceremony?"

"No," I said so forcefully she took a step back.

Richard's voice came out as little more than a whisper. "Is Hermes riding in a Baby Bjorn?"

"I got the baby carrier from the nice family on the second floor who no longer have babies," she told him. "Hermes loves it."

I crossed to Leatrice, giving Hermes a rub on the head. "You can't be here."

"But you need me, especially all the information I got on Tina Pink." Leatrice lifted Hermes out of the carrier and handed him to Richard, who still looked gob-smacked. "You were right; she has reason to want to get revenge on all of you."

CHAPTER 24

"All of us?" Fern asked as he rubbed Hermes under the chin.

"Weren't you all responsible for what happened to her husband?" Leatrice asked, unhooking the baby carrier from around her waist and lifting it over her shoulders.

"What is she wearing?" Richard whispered to me.

Without the baby carrier covering her chest, I got a full view of Leatrice's bright flower-print dress with puffy sleeves. So much for her flying under the radar.

Mack set his spray bottles on the counter. "But it was self-defense."

"I doubt Tina Pink sees it that way." Leatrice shuffled to the glass wall overlooking the terrace and pool. "Did you know her big house was repossessed as well as her fancy cars? And all her bank accounts were frozen."

I swallowed hard. "So she went from being a wealthy Potomac wife to having nothing?"

"Maybe she shouldn't have married a criminal," Richard said. "I hope I'm not supposed to have sympathy for her."

"We shouldn't judge until we've walked a mile in the other person's shoes," Mack said.

Richard wrinkled his nose. "Wear someone else's shoes? Not unless they're the new Prada loafers, honey."

Hermes yipped in agreement.

Leatrice spotted Daniel, and her bright-coral mouth curled into a smile. "You look familiar." Her smile faltered. "You never appeared on *America's Most Wanted*, did you?"

"No," Daniel said, holding out his hand. "I'm Daniel Reese. Mike's brother."

"Of course." Leatrice ignored his extended hand and gave him a hug. "I can see the family resemblance." She darted a glance at his ring finger. "And you're not married either I see."

Daniel stammered while his brother looked on, grinning.

"So what has she been doing?" I asked, trying to steer the conversation back to Tina. "She disappeared from the wedding scene, and I assumed she left town. Even her BFF Brianna pretended she'd never heard of her."

"Typical Brianna," Fern said. "That wedding planner doesn't have a loyal bone in her body."

"You know she interviewed for this wedding," I said.

"You went up against Brides by Brianna to get the Hamilton wedding?" Richard looked over his shoulder. "Are we sure she isn't here with Tina trying to ruin us?"

Fern shuddered. "Don't even joke."

"From what my online buddies could find, Ms. Pink is living in a rented studio apartment somewhere near Mount Vernon," Leatrice said.

I wondered if these were the same online buddies from Leatrice's days hanging out on the dark net with hackers named Dagger Dan and Boots. After getting me in trouble for using her hacked information, and after her online pals had gone underground for a while, she'd agreed not to dabble in the quasi-legal. I suspected she occasionally used her buddies for intel, although she never admitted it, and I didn't ask. Some things I'd rather not know.

Richard shook his head. "How the mighty have fallen."

"Okay," I said, pacing small circles as I thought out loud. "She loses everything, blames us, and comes up with a plan to crash one of our big weddings and kidnap Kate."

Mack sucked in a breath. "I'll bet she heard about the wedding from Brianna."

"You know," I said, "you may be on to something. We booked this wedding before everything went down with Tina, which means she and Brianna were still buds. I'll bet Brianna mentioned losing this wedding to us and probably gave all the details to her friend without knowing it. The Hamiltons had the date and location settled before they interviewed planners. That would explain how Tina knew enough to infiltrate the event."

"This is all well and good," Richard said. "But we don't know for sure if Tina Pink is here or behind everything."

"Then who were we chasing?" I asked.

"A terrified waiter?" Richard suggested. "Tell me this, darling, how would Tina know enough about Mr. Hamilton's work to ask for his nerve agent as ransom?"

I gave Richard an exasperated sigh. "Maybe she researched his pharma company and came up with the ransom scheme. Aren't you always admonishing me for not learning more about my clients? It's possible she found out about the DOD contract and concocted the plan from there."

Richard gave me a look that told me he wasn't convinced, but before I could argue with him any further, Reese put a hand on my arm.

"The first thing we need to do is track down this woman." He twisted to face me. "You say she's still blond but her hair is cut like a man's, right?"

"Yes," I said. "And she's wearing black pants, a white shirt, and a long bistro apron like the rest of the waiters."

"This shouldn't be too hard," Fern said. "Most of Richard's waiters are tall, dark, and hunky. From what I remember, Tina is a string bean."

Leatrice rubbed her hands together. "I love a good search."

I took another look at her boldly patterned dress, the fabric shiny and the puffy sleeves larger than her head. "I can't have you wandering around like that."

Leatrice dropped her eyes to her dress. "This is the dress I wore to the last wedding I attended. You don't like it?"

"You haven't been to a wedding since the Reagan administration?" Richard asked, reaching out to touch the floral print fabric like it was radioactive.

"Not unless you count the wedding you planned on the yacht," she said. "And at that wedding, I wasn't dressed as a guest since I was helping you track down a killer."

"No, you weren't." No amount of hypnotherapy could remove the image of Leatrice in a sailor suit. "But I can't pass you off as a guest since the guests aren't here yet, and the family is crawling all over the place."

Richard tapped his chin with one finger. "We could hide her in a closet."

I took Leatrice by the elbow and leveled a finger at Richard. "I'm going to put her in a costume. You'd better figure out how to explain Hermes."

Richard looked down at the tiny dog squirming in his arms. Hermes wiggled up to lick his chin and yipped.

"The rest of us will spread out and look for Tina Pink," Reese said. "Don't try to apprehend her on your own. Text me, and Daniel and I will come to you. I don't want anyone trying to be a hero." He leaned down close to my ear. "Especially you, babe."

I felt chills travel down my spine, and I couldn't stop my eyes from lingering on his backside as he and Daniel headed outside. I looked away quickly when Richard caught me staring.

"I'll go tell Buster," Mack said. "He still holds a grudge against her for stealing away one of our best employees."

"I thought to forgive was the Christian thing to do," I teased. "Tina isn't on your prayer list?"

Mack picked up his spray bottles on his way out of the kitchen and paused in the doorway. "Oh, she is. Buster prays she'll get what's coming to her."

"Now that's the kind of praying I can get behind," Fern said after Mack had left the room. "Maybe I should start going to their prayer meetings." He smoothed the shoulders of his black-and-white-striped top. "In the meantime, I'm going to search upstairs and finish the bridesmaids' hair."

As he sashayed out of the kitchen, I tried to imagine the prim hairstylist at one of the gatherings of the Road Riders for Jesus, but the thought of Fern in leather and chains made my head hurt.

"Come on." I pulled Leatrice with me toward the French doors. "The costumes are in the pool house."

"Wait for me." Richard hurried after us, his dog jiggling in his arms. "Maybe I can find something for Hermes to wear."

I highly doubted Sidney Allen stocked dog-sized costumes, but I didn't want to burst Richard's bubble. We skirted the length of the pool with me pulling Leatrice by the sleeve to speed up her pace. I wanted to spend the least amount of time possible outside in the heat, even though I suspected it was a lost cause and my makeup had melted off ages ago. We reached the pool house, which had glass-paned French doors exactly like the ones on the main house.

"I've never been in a pool house before," Leatrice said as I opened the door and ushered her inside. "Is this where the pool boy lives?"

"Pool boy?" Richard gave her the side-eye. "Have you been watching reruns of *Desperate Housewives* again?"

"It's where people change into suits or shower after they've been swimming," I explained, stepping aside for a man in a red page boy costume trimmed in gold braid to pass by.

Leatrice gaped at the main room of the pool house with its wet bar to one side, pair of sofas covered in pale-green twill and piled with striped cushions, and flat-screen TV mounted on the wall. "They have a separate house for that?"

"Yes, but it's normally not this chaotic."

A metal garment rack, holding costumes in a range of colors from burgundy to black to ivory, stood to one side of the wet bar. Plastic dry cleaning bags and duffels littered the couches and floor. People milled about the space, some of them in elaborate Venetian garb, and some barely wearing anything at all. The trays of food on the wet bar had been decimated, and small glass soda bottles filled the trash can next to one of the sofas.

I didn't hear or see Sidney Allen, so I made a beeline for the costume rack, pawing through the options until I found one I thought would fit and wouldn't be missed. I pulled out the green-and-purple outfit and handed it to Leatrice. "Try this on."

"I like the colors," she said. "And the bells."

I pointed her to the bathroom down the short hallway so she could change in private.

"A jester?" Richard said, flicking through the costumes himself. "Appropriate."

"It's one of the only ones that won't dwarf her," I said. "Plus, it won't kill us to have one less jester in the official wedding performances."

"Tell that to Sidney Allen," Richard muttered.

I jerked my head around. "Do you see him? Is he coming?"

"No, but you know he'll have a fit when another of his costumes goes missing."

Richard was right. Sidney Allen had never under reacted to anything in his life, nor would he have any interest in hearing why I'd borrowed the costume.

"I haven't seen or heard him in a while," I said, plucking one of the last bottles of Sprite from the counter. "I've never known him to keep a low profile during setup."

"No one knows where he is," a man in a gold-and-black mask and a black bodysuit said from where he sat on a couch.

"What do you mean?" I asked, taking a sip of Sprite and wishing it was cold.

The man slid the mask to the top of his head. "He's supposed to come in and make final adjustments to our costumes and go over our places, but we've been waiting for close to an hour."

I exchanged a glance with Richard, whose eyebrows had popped up.

"Has this ever happened before?" I asked the performer.

"Never," he said. "I've worked with Sidney for a year, and he's always on top of things. Sometimes too much, if you know what I mean."

I did.

"I went to look for him." A woman in a full satin skirt the color of champagne and tight lace-up bodice flopped down beside the man in black. "Couldn't find the little guy anywhere."

"So we have two people kidnapped, another attacked, missing costumes, and now a missing entertainment diva?" Richard said.

"That's what he was doing the last time I saw him." The woman loosened her laces and let out a breath. "Looking for his missing costumes."

"Maybe he found them," Richard said, "and stumbled onto something he shouldn't have."

The feeling of dread turned into a knot in my stomach. If Reese was right and all the mishaps were connected, Sidney Allen's search for his costumes could be more dangerous than he knew. "And now he's missing too."

CHAPTER 25

"*W*ell," Leatrice said, stepping out of the bathroom, the bells on her jester costume jingling. "What do you think?"

I appraised my octogenarian neighbor. The shiny satin outfit consisted of puffy pantaloons that reached almost to her shins, even though I knew they were meant to hit above the knee. The ruff around her neck had layers of stiff fabric points in the same multicolored diamond pattern with bells at the tips.

Richard tapped his finger to his bottom lip. "With the hat, she's almost the size of a normal person."

The hat, which resembled a diamond-patterned pineapple bursting open on her head, did give her an extra six inches at least. Leatrice straightened the hat and looked to Richard and me with an eager expression on her wrinkled face.

"I think you look great, Leatrice," I said and drained the last of my Sprite, desperately wishing the bottles caterers set out for vendors weren't the short squat ones that were empty after a few gulps.

Leatrice jerked a thumb toward the bathroom door she'd exited. "Should I be concerned that there are two penguins splashing around in the bathtub?"

160

That answered one of my questions. I noticed the penguin handler leaning up against a wall, scrolling on her phone.

"Not in the least," I said. "The heat outside must have gotten to them."

Leatrice tapped a finger to the side of her face. "You don't think our building would allow penguins as pets, do you?"

"I'm pretty sure that's a no," I said. I did not want to imagine Leatrice walking a pair of penguins down the streets of Georgetown.

"Speaking of pets, what do we do with Hermes?" Richard asked, holding up the wriggling dog. "Sidney Allen has nothing for pint-sized performers."

"Too bad we didn't require children performers today," I said.

Richard shifted Hermes from one arm to the other. "Children aren't Lilliputians, Annabelle. Even a costume for a child would be too big for a tiny dog."

"I can wear him in the baby carrier again," Leatrice said.

"No," Richard and I said at the same time.

"It wouldn't go with your costume," I said, my voice softer. "And we want you to blend in with the rest of the performers."

"Good thinking." Leatrice nodded at me. "Shall we join the search? I may not know this Tina woman we're looking for, but how hard can it be to find a blonde with a boy-cut hairdo dressed up like a waiter?"

My eyes drifted to the rack of costumes and the two garishly outfitted performers reclined on the sofa. "Unless she's no longer dressed like a waiter."

Richard followed my gaze. "You aren't thinking what I think you're thinking?"

"She could easily have found a costume and be sneaking around the property as a performer and not a waiter," I said. "It would be a better disguise, especially since she's been made."

"To be clear," Richard held up a finger, "you're the only person who made her."

"She doesn't know that. She only knows we were both chasing her." I gave my best friend a pointed look. "She has no idea my friends would doubt my word and judgment."

Richard put both hands over his heart. "You wound me, darling."

"I believe you," Leatrice said, bouncing on the balls of her feet and her bells ringing. "Your instinct has been right on cases before. If you say your nemesis is here and is behind Kate's disappearance, then I say we go after her." She lowered her voice and leaned closer to me. "I've been reading up on advance interrogation techniques when we get to that point, dear."

"Heaven preserve us," Richard said under his breath.

"If you think Tina will be in her waiter uniform," I told Richard, "why don't you take the lead on checking with your wait staff? Ask them if they've seen someone who fits her description, and see if she's hanging out in the catering kitchen or the tents. It will make more sense coming from you anyway."

Richard tucked Hermes under his arm like a football. "You're right, of course. If anyone should question my waiters, it should be me. And being in the catering kitchen and tents will keep me and, most importantly, Hermes out of sight of the family."

He left the pool house with Hermes's tail poking out from under his arm and swishing back and forth like a furry windshield wiper.

"What about me?" Leatrice rubbed her hands together.

Not only was Leatrice unfamiliar with the house and grounds, she had a propensity for getting herself in trouble when left alone. I did not want her wandering around by herself since multiple people were now missing and one person had been attacked.

"You and I are going to look for Sidney Allen," I said. "If he really is missing, he could be in danger."

"Who is Sidney Allen?" Leatrice asked, following me outside the pool house.

I pulled the French door closed behind me and immediately missed the air conditioning. Even though it was now late afternoon, the heat was slow to dissipate, and I felt beads of sweat gather on my upper lip.

"He's the man who provided all the costumed performers. He owns a specialty entertainment company and is the person to see if

you want Cirque du Soleil-style acrobats or royal family imperson-
ators at your event."

Leatrice scratched the side of her head where her hat had slipped
down. "And people want those types of things at weddings?"

"Not usually," I admitted as I led the way across the pool deck
toward the house, casting a glance down the hill at the empty ceremony tent. "It's a niche market, but he does a good corporate business. Big companies love splashy entertainment at their galas. At
weddings, most brides don't want anything that will upstage them."

"So you don't work with him often?" Leatrice hurried along
behind me and jingled as she ran, giving me the uncanny feeling I was
being chased by Santa's sleigh.

"No. He's a bit of a handful himself, so he's not one of my usual
vendors." I paused at the door leading into the house, peering into the
kitchen and casual dining room for any family members. "But this
wedding called for it."

Leatrice glanced back at the reception tent with the hanging
chandeliers and towering floral arrangements rising from the tables
to meet them. "I can see that. Is the bride famous?"

I shook my head. "Her father is wealthy."

"And that's why she was kidnapped?" Leatrice asked as I opened
the glass door and stepped into the house. "For the money?"

"Not exactly," I said. I knew Leatrice was dying to know all the
juicy details, but now that Tina Pink was in play, I wasn't even sure
Mr. Hamilton's nerve gas had anything to do with it. "If I'm right
about Tina Pink, everything will make sense soon enough. Right now
we need to find Sidney Allen and make sure he's okay."

"Why do you think he wouldn't be?" Leatrice said as we passed
through the kitchen and into the expansive marble foyer.

"Sidney Allen isn't someone who's easy to miss," I explained. "If he
was here, we would know it. He would be squawking about us
running late or complaining about his missing costumes or something. He's extremely detail oriented and lets you know the second
something isn't perfect. The fact that no one has seen him and we
can't hear him means something is wrong."

"Maybe we should try to retrace his steps."

"Good idea," I said, opening the heavy front door and poking my head outside to the empty driveway. No Sidney. "Except we have no idea of his steps."

I closed the front door and wondered if I should bother searching upstairs. I doubted Sidney would have ventured to the client's private bedrooms. Sidney might have been high-maintenance, but he worshipped at the Southern altar of propriety and good manners.

Leatrice tapped her foot and the ringing echoed off the floor. I noticed her matching shoe had an upturned toe topped with a bell. "If you wanted to stash something in this house, where would you do it?"

I thought for a moment. "There are a ton of closets. I'd probably throw it in one of them."

Leatrice stuck one hand in the air. "Lead on to the closets."

I made my way down the hallway leading to the garage, opening a coat closet and finding nothing but coats and a substantial collection of golf umbrellas. I passed the open door to Sherry's office where Daniel sat next to the injured woman, along with Aunt Connie and the brunette bridesmaid I now knew was Sherry's daughter. I rushed Leatrice by the doorway when she slowed to get a better look. "I'll explain later," I whispered.

I flattened Leatrice against the wall as a procession of half a dozen performers in burgundy cloaks and white masks passed us coming from the garage-turned-catering-kitchen. "Three more closets on this hall," I said once they'd passed. "Then we can check the garage."

Leatrice didn't respond, and I could feel she was no longer behind me, so I turned to see that she'd fallen in step behind the row of masks and was following them toward the foyer. What on earth was she doing? I hissed her name, but she didn't seem to hear me. If I spoke any louder, everyone from Sherry's office would hear me, so I ran on tiptoes to catch up with Leatrice, hoping to reach her before any of the masked performers noticed a jingling jester behind them.

As I reached her and was about to grab her by the arm, Leatrice stepped down on the hem of the last masked performer's cloak. The wearer jerked back, and I heard a distinctly female string of curses emerge from underneath the shiny white face mask.

I gasped as I recognized the voice, stepping past Leatrice and pulling the mask off to reveal Tina Pink. Her face was flushed, and her eyes burned with hatred. She caught me off guard with a hard slap to the cheek, and my eyes watered from the impact.

"Cheese and crackers!" I couldn't see Mack, but I'd recognize his own version of expletives anywhere. "Annabelle was right. It's Tina Pink."

"And she's making a run for it," Leatrice said.

I blinked a few times until I could focus on the still-cloaked figure dashing through the doorway to the kitchen. "Oh, no you don't." I took off after her, holding my stinging cheek and wondering how many rings she'd been wearing when she hit me.

I heard Mack behind me, as well as Leatrice's tinkling bells, as we ran through the kitchen, around the table, and out the French doors. Tina Pink had dropped her cloak in a pile on the pool deck and was only a few feet ahead of us, but her long legs were gaining ground as she tore around the pool. I pumped my legs harder as I tried to catch her, grateful my black dress did not have a straight skirt.

I saw a flash of black-and-white stripes as Fern opened the door to the pool house, and it smacked Tina square in the face, sending her flying backward with her hands clutching her nose. She stumbled back and fell onto a lounge chair, blood gushing from between her fingers as she let out a string of profanity. Hermes scampered up yipping wildly, and I turned to see Richard crossing the reception tent after him.

"What on earth?" Richard was breathing hard when he reached me. "Hermes heard something and jumped out of my arms." He looked at the bloody blonde and his eyes widened. "Is that?"

"Tina Pink." I put my hands on my knees and sucked in air. "Like I told you."

Hermes circled the lounge chair where she sat moaning and holding her clearly broken nose. He growled at her when she made a move to get up, and Mack clamped a heavy hand onto her shoulder.

Reese appeared at my side, breathing like he'd been running as well. "I saw you all from an upstairs window. Is that who I think it is?"

"I caught her disguised as a masked something-or-other," Leatrice said, beaming up at the detective.

"How did you know it was her?" I asked.

"She was taller than the other people in the line," my neighbor said. "If your friend Sidney is as precise as you say he is, I didn't think he'd have one person stick out so much from the rest."

"Good eyes." Reese patted her on the back. "You would have made a decent detective."

Leatrice's cheeks turned pink, and I thought there was a fair chance she might faint from the compliment.

Reese looked at me. "What happened to you?"

I put a hand to my cheek again and felt a trickle of blood. "She hit me, and I think this is courtesy of a big ring."

Reese brushed his thumb against my cheek. "I don't think you'll scar."

"You still came out ahead." Richard looked at Tina and the blood dripping down her face.

"It's too late, you know." Tina looked up at us, her words coming out in angry bursts. "It's already done."

"What do mean 'it's already done'?" I asked, meeting her angry gaze. "Did you kill them?"

Her eyes flickered. "Kill them? What are you talking about?"

"Kate and the bride," I said. "You kidnapped them. What have you done with them?"

"I didn't kidnap your stupid assistant." Tina struggled fruitlessly under Mack's grasp.

"Kate is not stupid," Richard said, reaching down to pat Hermes on the head and quiet him. "She's unencumbered by intellectualism."

I wasn't sure that was the compliment Richard thought it was.

"I don't believe you," I said. "You want me to believe you just happen to be here when Kate is kidnapped?"

"Believe what you want, but my goal for today was to make this wedding one no guest would ever forget," she said, her voice muffled by her hands. "Especially when they all got violently ill with food poisoning."

"What?" Richard's voice was almost inaudible.

Tina focused on Richard. "That's right. I've been in your kitchen all day adding special ingredients to your food."

Richard let out a high-pitched shriek. "My historically accurate canapés! My squid ink risotto!" He took off running for the garage, arms waving over his head and Hermes on his heels.

Tina met Reese's eyes. "I remember who you are, handsome. You can arrest me for tampering with the food, but I had nothing to do with the kidnapping. Not that I don't want to tip my hat to whoever did it."

I wasn't sure if I believed her, but I also didn't know if I truly believed she could have pulled off the kidnapping solo. I felt a wave of panic as I realized we were back to square one. If Tina didn't kidnap Kate and Veronica, who did?

CHAPTER 26

"*D*o you believe her?" I asked Reese as we traipsed back to the house, Mack still prodding Tina along in front of us.

"She looked genuinely surprised to be accused of kidnapping, although she could be an excellent actress," Reese said. "And I don't know why she'd orchestrate a kidnapping and ransom drop and still be here. Either she's part of a multi-person plot, or she's doing what she says she was—trying to sabotage the wedding."

"That reminds me," I looked toward the tents and garage, "I should check on Richard at some point. If all his food really is ruined, he's going to be beside himself."

Leatrice slow jogged beside us to keep up, and her bells shook with every bounce. "If the food is ruined, what will he do for the wedding?"

I spread my arms wide. "What wedding? We still don't have a bride, and her father paid the ransom a while ago. Either something went wrong with the drop, or our suspicions were right and this wasn't about the ransom in the first place."

Leatrice slowed. "What does that mean for Kate?"

I bit the edge of my bottom lip and told myself crying wouldn't help anything. Reese took my hand in his and squeezed.

"It's past time to bring in the police," Reese said, holding up a hand when I opened my mouth to say he was police. "In an official capacity."

My shoulders slumped as the reality sank in. Kate and the bride had been missing for hours. The ransom had been delivered, yet they hadn't been returned. Tina Pink probably didn't have anything to do with it, even though she was the reason no one would be eating. The wedding I'd worked on for over a year was a total disaster and would be the only wedding to date we'd have to call off. I prided myself in never having had a bride or groom left at the altar or even a wedding cancelled at the last minute. Now that was probably out the window, along with my assistant's chances for being returned safely.

I pressed a hand to my mouth as I felt the tears I'd been holding back all day spill out onto my cheeks. Reese wrapped me in his arms, stopping outside the French doors and letting everyone else go ahead in without us. His arms felt solid around me, making me feel safe and making me cry even harder. I felt my resolve slip away as fear and regret washed over me.

"This is my fault," I said through sobs. "I should have listened to you at the beginning and let the cops come in. If something happens to Kate . . ."

Reese shushed me and rubbed my back. "You were going along with what the kidnappers said. You did what you did because you were trying to keep her safe."

"But what if I was wrong?" I gazed up at him through blurry eyes. "What if it put Kate and Veronica in more danger? You're right that I'm always trying to fix things myself, which is exactly what I did here."

Reese brushed a few tears off my face. "Not exactly. You called me in right away."

"And convinced you not to call in backup." I wiped at my nose.

"But I didn't listen to you and called my brother." He grinned at me. "See? We're both pretty stubborn and used to doing things our own way."

I leaned my head against his shoulder. "I promise if we get Kate back safely, I will never try to do your job again."

Reese laughed. "Bold words from someone who's been poking her nose into my cases since the day we met. I don't think you could stop yourself if your life depended on it."

I started to argue with him, realized he was right, and felt myself smiling despite my best efforts not to. "You don't have much faith in my ability to change."

"Why would I want you to change?" he asked. "I love you exactly the way you are, crazy meddling and crazy friends included."

I stopped breathing for a moment as I realized he'd just told me he loved me for the first time. Not quite the romantic setting I'd envisioned for such a declaration, but nothing about our relationship had been as I'd have planned it. Maybe having something in my life I didn't plan wasn't such a bad thing.

I wrapped my arms around his waist. "I love you too. Despite the fact that you *don't* have any crazy friends."

"I'll share yours. You have plenty to spare." He ran a finger along my jawline and tilted my face up to his, leaning down to kiss me lightly. My pulse quickened, and I felt like I was in danger of crying again. Happy tears this time.

Throat clearing from the French doors pulled me back to reality. I opened my eyes and looked behind me to see Fern smirking at me with his arms crossed. "I hate to interrupt, but what are we doing with Tina? She's not exactly keeping a low profile in here."

I could hear her loud voice from outside. Even if she wasn't responsible for the kidnapping, she was responsible for sabotaging the wedding and needed to be questioned by the authorities. We would have to call the police, and I would have to explain things to the Hamiltons. I drew a breath to steady myself.

"Can you call the cops to come get Tina while I break the news to the parents?" I asked Reese.

"Sure." He pulled his phone out of his pocket. "But are you sure you don't want me to talk to them with you?"

"You're supposed to be a sommelier, remember?" I grinned at him.

"I don't want to have to explain that lie along with everything else. Besides, you and Richard are such a cute couple."

He gave me a look. "I'm going to let that slide since you've had a rough day."

"Look on the bright side," I said. "I think he's warming up to you."

"Really?" Reese asked, his face eager. "How long until you think he actually likes me?"

I pondered for a moment. "Five years tops."

Reese sighed. "That's encouraging."

We joined everyone in the kitchen where Tina sat at the oval table holding a dish towel to her nose with Mack, arms crossed, standing behind her. Her scowl seemed permanent, but her previously defiant posture had wilted as she slumped down in the chair.

Buster had joined the group and had obviously been brought up to speed. He stood next to Mack with his hands on his hips glaring down at Tina with such menace I actually felt bad for her.

"So you're going to keep me here all night?" Tina asked, her voice nasal.

"No," I said. "We're going to have the police haul you away. Attempting to poison two hundred people is a pretty serious matter."

"It wasn't real poison," Tina said. "No one would have died."

I bobbed my shoulders up and down. "That's up to the police to determine. And the Hamiltons when they press charges."

Tina sagged further. "All I wanted was for you all to get some payback for ruining my life."

"We didn't ruin your life," I said. "You did that all on your own by marrying a criminal."

"Maybe if you stopped blaming other people for your bad decisions, you wouldn't be heading off to prison as well," Mack added.

"Do they have his-and-hers prisons?" Fern asked.

Leatrice shook her head, and the bells on her hat jingled.

"What's going on here?" Daniel asked as he and Alexandra entered the room.

"We caught this one wearing a disguise," Leatrice said, jerking a thumb toward Tina.

"I'm assuming this is the rival wedding planner?" Daniel asked.

"We don't think she was involved in the kidnapping," Reese said. "But she admitted to tampering with the food for the wedding so all the guests would get food poisoning."

Alexandra's eyes flew to the towering wedding cake on the wheeled table off to one side. "You don't think she . . .?"

Tina looked up and followed Alexandra's eyes to the elaborately designed cake. "I didn't touch your cake."

Alexandra put the back of her hand to her forehead. "That's a relief."

"Especially since cake may be the only thing guests will have to eat," I said. "That is, if we're going to have a wedding at all."

"No word about Kate?" Alexandra asked. "Or Victoria?"

"Veronica?" I gave a quick shake of my head. "They should have been returned by now."

"We're sure *she* didn't have anything to do with it?" Buster's deep voice made Tina jump as he directed his gaze toward her. "Or the assistant being attacked?"

"Or the entertainment fellow disappearing?" Leatrice said.

Tina sat up. "Wait a minute. I don't know about any of those things. You can't pin all that on me."

"Depends," Daniel said, sitting down next to Tina. "Do you have any medical training?"

She looked at him like he'd taken leave of his senses. "What? No." Her eyes darted around the room. "What's going on? What is this about? I've copped to the food poisoning, but that's all I've done."

"What is this about?" Reese asked his brother.

Daniel stood again. "I checked on Sherry. She's not unconscious because she was knocked out. She's unconscious because she's been sedated."

"What?" I rubbed my temple. "But she has a knot on her forehead."

"She might have been knocked out originally," Daniel went on. "But I suspect it was done by someone who knew exactly how hard to hit her so she wouldn't be seriously injured. From the dilation of her pupils, I think she's been sedated to keep her from waking up and telling us who did it or what she knows."

"Well it wasn't me." Tina folded her arms across her chest. "I don't know anything about sedating someone and I hate needles."

I knew now it *wasn't* her.

CHAPTER 27

*R*eese slipped his cell phone back into his pants pocket. "Officers are on the way."

We were standing outside the front of the house so none of the family members would overhear the call and to get away from the hostility radiating off Tina. Despite the fact she'd been the one to sneak into the wedding and purposefully try to harm two hundred plus wedding guests, you'd have thought she was a freedom fighter being unjustly persecuted. Not that Buster and Mack were having any of it as they watched over her in the kitchen until the police arrived.

"I should talk to the parents before they hear the sirens," I said, reluctant to go back inside.

I let myself soak in the relative quiet of the bubbling marble fountain and empty driveway. I knew all the action was taking place right around the corner of the house where the tents were set up and trucks backed up to the garage, but for now I was happy to be removed enough to hear birds singing instead of a band doing sound checks. I allowed myself a breath—the scent of freshly mowed grass mingled with the scent of roses in the floral arrangements Buster and Mack had placed on either side of the front doors. I reached out and touched a white flower petal. Would anyone ever get to see the breathtaking decor we'd spent a year planning?

I brushed the thought from my mind. If we got Kate back, I wouldn't care about getting the wedding featured in a magazine or on a blog. Those things had never mattered to me much before, and after today, they'd fallen even farther down my list of priorities. For me, wedding planning was about relationships, not showing off. Sure, I'd done some pretty spectacular weddings, but it was the friends I'd made along the way that really mattered. I felt a surge of affection for the cast of characters I'd chosen to surround myself with and felt certain no one had better or more loyal friends.

"I should also check on Richard." I cast a look toward the side of the house leading to the garage and his makeshift kitchen. "I haven't seen him since he discovered Tina ruined his food. There's a decent chance he's slipped into a catatonic shock."

Reese put a hand on my waist. "I'll check on Richard and make sure he's okay."

"Really?" I asked. "You know he might be a bit unhinged and hysterical."

"Are you telling me the Richard I've seen is not him unhinged and hysterical?" Reese winked at me. "I've dealt with hardened criminals, babe. I'll be fine. Unless you want me to come with you and talk to the parents?"

"No." I waved him off. "I'll do it. I don't want to get into who you really are with them. At least until we have to."

He leaned down and kissed me on the forehead. "If you need me, you know where I'll be." He took a few steps backward, never breaking eye contact with me. "Either talking your best friend off the ledge or helping him cook dinner for two hundred."

He turned, and I watched him go, taking a moment to appreciate the view as he walked away. I gave myself a mental shake, reminding myself that there was no rest for the not very wicked and headed back into the house and toward Mr. Hamilton's study. I'd start with the father and move on to the mother. I tapped on the wooden door and poked my head inside. To my surprise, both parents were still in the study where I'd last seen them, although Tarek Nammour was no longer there.

Mr. Hamilton sat behind his large desk, his head in his hands as he leaned on his elbows. His wife paced the floor in front of him, wringing her hands and muttering to herself. I knew this was not the best time, but I also knew they would soon see flashing lights outside their home.

"Mr. and Mrs. Hamilton?" I said, stepping inside the room. "I hate to disturb, but I need to update you on a few things."

Mrs. Hamilton spun around. "Is it Veronica? Is she back?"

"No," I said quickly, not wanting to give her false hope. "If you don't mind me asking, where is Mr. Nammour?"

"Back home with his wife, I suppose," Mrs. Hamilton said, the bitterness in her voice unmistakable.

"If the security team let him leave," I said, wondering if the man wasn't in fact being held at the front gate.

"They know him," Mrs. Hamilton said. "He has the same company provide security for him."

If this kept up, I was going to need a chart to keep all the connections straight.

"Is that why you told me to hire them?" her husband asked, red creeping up his neck.

I jumped in before they started going at each other again. "I wanted to let you know we found someone trying to sabotage the wedding, and we're turning her over to the police."

Mr. Hamilton looked up, his face ashen. "Is this connected to the kidnapping?"

"We don't think so, no."

"What is happening?" The bride's mother threw her hands in the air. "Veronica gets kidnapped, Sherry gets attacked, and someone tries to ruin the wedding? My husband delivered the ransom. This should all be over."

"This was never about the ransom or the nerve gas," I said. "Everything that's happened today was personal."

I didn't add that even Tina's sabotage was personally motivated against my friends and me.

Mrs. Hamilton's eyes snapped to me. "What do you mean?"

"If this was about the ransom, Veronica and my assistant would have been returned once it was delivered. But they weren't because it was about making you suffer, Mr. Hamilton. Someone knocked out Sherry but didn't kill her and has kept her sedated so she can't talk. A terrorist would have killed her without a second thought."

"What?" Mrs. Hamilton staggered back into a leather chair.

"I think all this has to do with what someone in this family is hiding." I stared pointedly at the bride's father.

"It's all my fault," Mr. Hamilton said and put his head back in his hands. "You were right about me, Deborah. I've ruined this family with my secrets and lies."

Now we were getting somewhere.

"It's not only you." Mrs. Hamilton's voice barely reached a whisper. "I've been lying to you for over twenty years."

"You've been seeing Tarek for that long?" Mr. Hamilton glanced up, his eyes filled with tears.

His wife shook her head. "Not that. That doesn't mean anything. It was my way of getting back at you for all of your affairs over the years."

"Then what?" he asked.

She took a shaky breath. "I've been keeping your daughter from you."

He jerked upright in his chair. "You? You kidnapped Veronica?"

She held up her hands. "Not Veronica. Your other daughter. The one you didn't know you had."

Mr. Hamilton shook his head like he was trying to loosen something from inside. "What other daughter? You're not making any sense."

"I know about your fling with my sister when I was pregnant with Veronica. She told me the two of you got drunk one night when she was visiting us, and one thing led to another."

He blinked quickly. "That was over twenty years ago. I remember

Connie coming on to me one night, but I'd had a lot of wine." His voice rose. "How can she be sure it was mine? You know your sister got around."

"She had DNA tests done." Mrs. Hamilton's voice grew louder as well. "She showed me. The child was yours. I've been paying her ever since to keep her from telling our children."

He sank back into his desk chair. "Wait. Are you telling me . . .?"

"Cara isn't your niece," his wife said. "She's your daughter."

This I did not expect. I glanced at Mr. Hamilton's stunned expression and wondered if I looked the same.

Mr. Hamilton rubbed a hand across his furrowed forehead. "Does she know?"

"She has no idea," the bride's mother said. "That's part of the deal. I'd pay for everything, including her college, as long as she never knew."

"You'd pay?" Mr. Hamilton stood up. "With my money, you mean."

His wife stood up as well. "Yes, with your dirty money."

My mind raced with the new information. I remembered Aunt Connie's thinly veiled contempt for her sister's husband, as well as Sherry telling me about the mother's payouts to her. The house for the grandmother must have been another payoff if Connie told her mother. I wondered how much money had been spent to keep Mr. Hamilton's sordid secret and if this information was why Sherry had been silenced. Connie must have known she was chatty and also must have known she would have seen the family financials and either figured it out or been told by Mrs. Hamilton. And since Connie was a nurse, she could knock Sherry out and keep her sedated while pretending to take care of her.

"Mrs. Hamilton," I said, hearing the flutter of panic in my voice. "Where is your sister?"

The woman looked startled to see I was still in the room. "Connie. I don't know. Why?" She studied my face for a moment. "You don't think she . . ." Her hand flew to her mouth. "She wouldn't. She loves Veronica."

Even as she said it, I could tell she didn't believe her own words.

The realization that her sister had enough pent-up anger and resentment to hurt the daughter who had been acknowledged and loved while hers hadn't seemed to hit Mrs. Hamilton all at once. Her knees gave way, and she collapsed to the floor.

Her husband rushed around the desk and knelt down beside her. "Don't worry. I'll talk to Connie. I'll fix this. I'm sure she won't hurt Veronica. She just wants to punish us."

I turned to slip out of the room but was met with two men in dark suits. These guys weren't cops, I thought, as I sized them up.

They looked past me into the room. "We're looking for Stephen Hamilton."

Mr. Hamilton raised his eyes from his sobbing wife. "Who are you?"

One of the men stepped forward. "Sir, we're with the Department of Homeland Security."

As they moved past me into the room, I scooted out into the hallway. I needed to find Reese and Daniel right away and tell them everything. I headed back through the foyer, stopping short when I saw the grandmother holding open the front door for a stream of official looking men. She locked eyes with me—her expression steely —until she broke into a smile that made her look even more sinister. Not only did this woman seem unconcerned about her missing granddaughter, she appeared to be reveling in her son-in-law's and daughter's life unraveling. I felt a rush of gratitude that this wasn't my family as I continued walking quickly toward the garage where I knew Reese should be.

Leatrice caught up to me when I was only a few steps into the opposite hallway. She no longer wore her hat, but the bells on her costume still jingled enough to announce her presence behind me.

"There you are, dear," she said. "I've been searching everywhere for you."

"I'm on my way to find Reese," I said, not slowing down. "I think I know who took Kate and the bride."

"That's wonderful." Leatrice jogged beside me to keep up. "Are you still looking for the entertainment fellow?"

I slowed my pace. Even if I had a lead on Kate, Sidney Allen was still missing and, despite how much he annoyed me, I was worried no one had heard from him. "I haven't found him if that's what you're asking."

"I know that, dear," Leatrice said with a giggle. "Because I did. Find him, that is. At least I assume it's him. Would you say he's small enough to fit inside a dumbwaiter?"

CHAPTER 28

I wasn't sure I'd heard her correctly. "This house has a dumbwaiter?"

Leatrice bobbed her head up and down. "In that little hallway off the formal dining room. It seems to connect to the basement, but I personally haven't ridden it."

I wasn't completely surprised I hadn't noticed the dumbwaiter in the butler's walk-through pantry. I'd only passed through the space once or twice, and the mansion did have over thirty rooms.

"And you're saying a person is inside this dumbwaiter?" I asked.

"Yes, and the only way I noticed was the edge of his blazer wedged in the dumbwaiter door. Otherwise I never would have noticed there was a dumbwaiter in the first place. It's built seamlessly into the cabinets."

I sighed. Finding Reese and sharing my new theory with him would have to wait. As much as Sidney Allen annoyed me, I owed it to him not to leave him wedged inside a dumbwaiter. I did an about-face and headed toward the formal dining room with Leatrice by my side.

The lights were off in the long room, but the tall windows at one end let in enough remaining sunlight to illuminate the rectangular dining table surrounded by beige tufted chairs. Off to one side of the room was the butler's pantry leading into the casual dining room and kitchen. I pulled open the sliding door and flipped on the overhead pendant lights. The door at the other end of the walk-through space was closed, which was just as well. If Buster and Mack were still guarding Tina in the kitchen, I did not want to alert them to the possibility of a new homicide until I was certain.

Leatrice extended a finger. "Down there."

I glanced down the row of white cabinetry that ran from floor to ceiling and was broken up by an alabaster marble counter matching the one in the kitchen. The room held the distinct odor of lemon furniture polish and Windex, reminding me the Hamiltons' house-keepers had given the entire house a thorough cleaning the day before. At the end of the counter, I noticed a door hanging open and a flap of blue fabric hanging out. I steeled myself for the sight of Sidney Allen's dead body as I approached.

It was indeed Sidney Allen with his knees tucked up to his chest and his head resting on his hands. The space inside the dumbwaiter was larger than I'd expected, and even though the man was small in stature, I felt like I could have squeezed into the space if I'd tried hard enough.

"Sidney?" I reached out tentatively and felt his neck for a pulse, snatching my hand back when I realized he was actually alive. "Leatrice, he isn't dead. Let's get him out of here."

"I never said he was dead, dear," Leatrice said, as I wiggled Sidney's feet out. "Just that I'd found him."

I knew it wouldn't do any good to scold Leatrice for making me think the man had been killed. It was my fault for jumping to conclusions, although with my track record of finding dead bodies, who could blame me?

Leatrice helped me lower Sidney gently to the ground where I stretched him out and began gently patting his cheeks to rouse him. Sidney made a few noises as he came to, his eyes fluttering open and locking onto me.

"Is she gone?" he asked.

"Is who gone?" I exchanged a look with Leatrice, wondering if Sidney Allen had been hit on the head before being stuffed into the dumbwaiter.

"I was trying to get away from her, and I ran in here." He pushed himself up onto his elbows. "I noticed the door hadn't been closed all the way and figured I could hide inside until I was sure she'd gone."

"You weren't forced inside?" I asked. "You got in there voluntarily?"

He bobbed his head. "The only problem is there's no way to open the door from the inside, and I started to get light-headed." He touched his fingers to his forehead. "I must have passed out."

"You're lucky Leatrice happened by when she did and saw your blazer sticking out of the door, or you might have suffocated," I told him.

Sidney Allen focused his eyes on Leatrice and beamed. "You saved me."

"It was nothing." Leatrice blushed. "If you think about it, it's a design flaw not to have air holes inside."

"I doubt they expected someone to try to ride it," I muttered.

Sidney Allen looked more carefully at Leatrice. "You're wearing one of my costumes."

Leatrice's cheeks reddened even more under her coral blush. "I'm afraid I had to borrow it to blend in. I'm actually Annabelle's neighbor, but I'm here in a strictly undercover capacity."

Sidney Allen gave a wave of his hand. "You look wonderful. I insist you keep it."

Leatrice brushed her hand over the shiny rainbow-colored fabric. "I couldn't. This is much too fancy. It must have cost you a pretty penny."

Sidney Allen took her hand in his. "A trifle, my dear. It would make me happy to think of you wearing it."

Good lord, was he flirting with her? And was I mistaken, or was Leatrice simpering like a schoolgirl?

"Annabelle," Leatrice nudged me in the ribs as she giggled, "you didn't tell me how charming your friend is."

"Trust me, this is as much of a surprise to me as it is to you," I said, turning my attention back to Sidney Allen. "You said you were trying to get away from someone."

Sidney tore his eyes away from Leatrice. "As you well know, I was searching for my missing costumes." His eyes darted back to Leatrice. "Not yours. A pair of ornate doge costumes I had specially made."

"Dog costumes?" Leatrice said. "We were looking for those earlier for Hermes."

"Not dog," I said. "Doge. Rhymes with rose. They were early rulers of Venice and wore elaborate outfits."

Sidney looked momentarily confused, then continued. "These were white embroidered satin with feather detailing, and were one of a kind. I remembered seeing some of my performers riding in a golf cart earlier, but I'd been distracted and forgotten about it. I thought the people I saw were in white, though I couldn't be certain since I saw them so briefly. I did suspect there could be a connection. Plus, I'd searched everywhere else."

"Do these people have their own golf course?" Leatrice asked.

"No," I said, a little bell beginning to sound in the back of my mind. "But they have a lot of land and horses, so they have a couple of golf carts they drive around when they need to visit the barn."

I'd never personally ridden the golf carts, but I'd been at the house when Mrs. Hamilton and her daughters had been returning from time with their horses.

"I tracked down the golf carts, and sure enough, my hand-embroidered costumes were stuffed in the back storage compartment in one of them."

His face darkened. "Can you believe it? Someone has the nerve to wear my costumes on a joy ride and then ruins them by jamming them into a dirty storage space."

Leatrice shook her head. "How awful for you. Are the costumes salvageable?"

"I'm not sure," Sidney said. "As I was pulling them out, I happened to glance up into the cart's rearview mirror and see someone about to hit me with a pipe. I ducked out of the way and took off running before she could try again. I ran around the house to the front door and dashed inside and found the dumbwaiter."

"Where you almost killed yourself," I finished for him. "Did you recognize the woman who tried to knock you over the head?"

Sidney bit his lower lip. "I only saw her for a second and only reflected in the mirror, so I didn't get a good look. All I know is she has brown hair."

That narrowed it down to most of the women in the Hamilton family and half the bridesmaids. The only people it cleared were the surly grandmother, Sherry, and Tina Pink.

Leatrice put a hand under Sidney Allen's arm. "Would you like me to help you rescue your costumes?"

Sidney Allen's face lit up. "You'd do that for me?"

I hoped this was not what Reese and I sounded like. If it was, I owed everyone around me an apology.

"It's the least I can do after you gave me this outfit." Leatrice batted her eyelashes and one side stuck together.

"Costume," I corrected. I did not want her thinking this was a jumpsuit she could wear out in public.

"We'll have to go back to the golf cart to get them," Sidney Allen said, his voice hushed as if he was suggesting crossing the Gobi desert.

I tuned the pair out, hoping I was imagining the burgeoning romance taking place in front of me. I didn't know if I could handle Sidney Allen dating Leatrice and showing up at my apartment building. It was hard enough handling Leatrice on her own.

I stood up, leaving the two on the floor exchanging compliments. I needed to find Reese and tell him what I'd learned from the Hamiltons. From what information I'd gathered, it seemed like Aunt Connie could have been the one who orchestrated the kidnapping, attacked Sherry, and tried to attack Sidney Allen.

I put my hand in my pocket and ran my fingers over the gummy bear and bit of white fluff, pulling out both and looking down at them. I sucked in my breath so suddenly both Leatrice and Sidney stopped flattering each other and looked up at me.

"I think I know where Kate and the bride are being held."

CHAPTER 29

I left Leatrice and Sidney still openmouthed on the floor of the butler's pantry. I had to find Reese and tell him what I knew or at least thought I knew. I hadn't heard back from my text which meant either he had his phone muted, or he was busy coping with Richard's drama. I slid open the door connecting the butler's pantry to the casual dining room. Buster and Mack looked up at me from across the room where they stood guarding Tina Pink, their expressions telling me they'd never noticed the door I'd emerged from.

Alexandra stood by her cake, adjusting the sugar flowers around the base, and straightened when she saw me. "Where did you come from?"

I scanned the room and determined Reese and Daniel were not in it. I indicated the room behind me with a jerk of my head. "We found Sidney Allen."

"Was he missing?" Mack asked. "I thought we were doing an excellent job of avoiding him."

"He was hiding," I said. "It's a long story and I have to find Reese first, but if I'm right, Tina definitely didn't have anything to do with the kidnapping."

"Like I've been telling you," Tina grumbled through her bloody dish towel, giving Buster and Mack a sinister look. "Didn't you say the police were on their way?"

"They should be here soon," I said. "Don't tell me you're eager to be hauled off to jail."

Tina lifted the towel off her nose. "Anything is better than having these two pray over me."

"You should be so lucky," I told her. "If it were up to me, they'd be doing an exorcism on you."

Mack's eyes brightened. "We could always try one. What's the worst that could happen?"

Buster pulled out his phone. "Let me Google how to make holy water."

Tina made a small squeaking noise and slid further down in her chair.

Alexandra crossed the room to me and held out her open palm. "You look like you need these."

The scent of the sugar petals reached me before I even looked down to see the collection of loose gum paste rose petals in her hand. I took one thin, pale-pink petal and popped it in my mouth, letting the sweetness dissolve on my tongue. I'd spent many a wedding day munching on Alexandra's extra petals for the much-needed sugar rush. "Thanks. I needed that."

Alexandra looked past me into the butler's pantry. "Is it me or is your neighbor cozying up to Sidney Allen?"

I put up a hand. "I can only deal with one catastrophe at a time. Let me focus on getting Kate back first."

I opened one of the French doors leading outside. It would be quicker to run around the back of the house to reach the garage, and there would be less chance of running into family members or Homeland Security. I wondered if the men in dark suits had taken Mr. Hamilton in or if they were questioning him here. Between the police Reese had called and the Homeland Security team, we were about to be overrun with law enforcement.

My stomach tightened. We needed to locate Kate before the police arrived and added to the confusion.

I hurried along the side of the pool, crossed through the middle of the dinner tent—taking care to scoot around the dance floor instead of across it with my shoes—and broke into a jog as I turned the corner of the house closest to the garage. I stopped abruptly as I nearly crashed headfirst into Fern. He screamed and two bottles of champagne bobbled in his arms.

"You nearly scared the life out of me," he said.

I eyed the bottles with their yellow labels. "Didn't we talk about cutting back when you're working?"

"These aren't for me." Fern gave me a look that told me he was insulted by the suggestion or was trying to be. "Mrs. Hamilton has locked herself in her room and is insisting I bring her bubbly."

I guessed the appearance of Homeland Security hadn't gone over well with her. "I don't blame her for wanting to drink after everything I've learned."

"Sounds intriguing." Fern shifted the bottles, and I could tell his urgency to get to the mother of the bride had been forgotten. "Tell me everything, sweetie."

"I don't have time to go into it now, but I can fill you in on my theory on the way to rescue Kate."

"We're going to rescue her now?" The champagne bottles nearly slipped out of his grasp. "You know where she is?"

"I think so," I said. "At least I have a pretty good theory I'd like to test out."

He set the bottles on the ground. "Lead the way." He started following me, then ran back and picked up one bottle, shrugging at me when I gave him a look. "You know we'll want to celebrate when we find her."

We dashed around to the open three-car garage that had been converted into Richard's catering kitchen for the day. Bare rectangular tables were lined up in rows and interspersed with tall metal warming boxes and shiny chrome ovens. Usually the kitchen would be bustling with activity from the pantry cooks to the waiters, but the waiters stood clustered in a corner, and the cooks in their white jackets were outside the kitchen. I didn't see any food out on the tables, but the air still held the aroma of freshly baked bread, sweet butter, and grilled meat.

I spotted Richard in the middle of the room with his head chef, recognizable by his chef's hat and black chef's jacket. The two men were hunched over a table, and I heard the unmistakable sound of curse words strung together in an impressive and creative combination. Knowing Richard and his equally temperamental chef, it could be coming from either of them or both. I didn't see Reese, and I wondered if he'd been here already and decided Richard was too much to handle.

"Have you seen Reese?" I called out to Richard.

He rushed over to me, his face smudged with what looked like traces of flour and possibly soot. "She was telling the truth. I don't know if she got every single hors d'oeuvre and dish, but she tampered with enough to make the entire wedding dinner unsalvageable."

"How do you know?" I asked.

Richard indicated the waiters standing to one side looking slightly green and a few I hadn't noticed earlier lying on their stomachs in the nearby grass. "I had my staff taste test it."

I clasped his arm. "You poisoned your own staff on purpose?" I noticed Hermes lounging on a patch of grass near the recovering waiters. "You didn't give any to Hermes, did you?"

He gave me a scandalized look. "The idea! You know Hermes only eats organic."

"And the waiters?" I crossed my arms and drummed my fingers across them.

"Don't look at me like that," Richard said, pulling away from me. "You sound like Mike. Anyway, I'm paying the ones who volunteered to be taste testers time and a half."

"Mike?" I wasn't used to Richard calling him by his actual name. "He was here? Do you know where he went?"

"Did you hear me, Annabelle?" Richard put both hands on his hips. "No, Food."

"I heard you, but that's not as big of a problem as No. Bride." I checked my phone again, but Reese hadn't replied. Where was he? If I was right, I didn't want to wait another minute to go after Kate. "Actually, Fern and I are going to find Kate. Are you in?"

"You know where she is?" he asked.

"She has a theory," Fern said.

I looked back toward the recovering waiters and saw a golf cart parked near the grass. "Can anyone drive one of those things?"

Fern hurried over to the black-and-white cart and hopped in the driver's seat, setting the champagne bottle next to him. "I watched Kate do it in Bali. How hard can it be?"

Richard and I exchanged a glance. Kate had forced another cart off the road and almost crashed when she'd driven a golf cart. I hoped Fern wasn't planning to replicate the experience.

I got in next to Fern, and Richard took the wide back seat. Hermes ran up and jumped in his lap, his pink tongue sticking out as he panted eagerly.

"Does this thing have seat belts?" Richard asked as we lurched forward and he nearly pitched off the back, catching Hermes with one hand. "Or helmets?"

I directed Fern to a gravel path.

"We aren't leaving the property?" he asked as we bumped down the narrow lane and the tires kicked up pebbles behind us.

"I don't think Kate and Veronica were really and truly kidnapped," I said, holding onto the bar over my head to keep from falling out. "I think they were lured away from the house and taken there." I pointed to the barn in the distance. "Sidney Allen says he saw some of his performers riding around in a golf cart, and he thinks they were in white. Then we find a bit of white feather in front of the house where we found Kate's phone. And Sidney Allen's doge costumes disappear, and he finds them stuffed into the back of a golf cart."

Fern took his eyes off the path and we veered onto the grass. "Are you telling me the kidnappers work for Sidney Allen?"

I pointed his face straight ahead. "No. I think the kidnapper somehow dressed up Kate and Veronica and drove them to the barn in a golf cart. With the number of costumed performers and the amount of chaos during setup, it wouldn't stand out too much."

"Unless you're Sidney Allen," Richard said.

"For once, I'm glad Sidney Allen is so uptight," I said. "If he wasn't so obsessive, I might never have made the connection. If I'm right, terrorists had nothing to do with all of this; the nerve gas was never picked up from the ransom drop; and both women have been right here the entire time."

"Are you telling me the barn was never checked?" Richard asked, bouncing up and down in the back seat with Hermes tucked under his arm.

"It seems like a pretty major fail on the part of the dad's cracker-jack security team, but we all assumed they'd been whisked away by an international terrorist organization, when really this whole thing stems from family problems."

"Since when do people solve family drama by kidnapping each other?" Fern asked. "I've known some crazy rich people, but this is a whole other level."

I filled Fern and Richard in on the secret daughter Mrs. Hamilton had kept from her husband and how bitter her sister seemed at the mention of her brother-in-law.

"Let me get this straight." Fern turned his attention to me, and the golf cart veered off the path and onto the grass again. "Veronica's cousin is actually her half sister? But neither of them know?"

I put one hand on the wheel to steer the cart back on track. "According to Mrs. Hamilton. She's been paying her sister off for years to keep it under wraps."

Fern shook his head. "Imagine being pregnant with your first child, and your husband gets your own sister knocked up. If it wasn't her daughter that had been taken, I'd say Mrs. Hamilton was behind this."

"Don't forget the person also had to have knocked out Sherry, but not kill her, and keep her sedated," I said. "That fits with Aunt Connie being a nurse. I don't think she wanted to kill anyone, but she might have known Sherry knew too much of the family gossip and was bound to spill something important. So she bopped her on the head enough to stun her, then shot her up with something to keep her out of it and unable to talk to us."

"And she did all this to ruin her niece's wedding?" Richard asked.

"I think she wanted to ruin Mr. Hamilton. Having him steal some of his company's own highly classified nerve agent would not have gone unnoticed. I'm sure she knew about the DOD contract from her sister. It doesn't take an expert in government contracting to know that giving your top-secret product to potential terrorists would not turn out well for him. Homeland Security agents arrived at the house not fifteen minutes ago."

"Talk about biting the hand that feeds you." Fern pressed his foot down on the accelerator as we approached the barn. "Didn't all the money that supported her daughter come from the man she just took down?"

I shrugged. "The daughter is grown up. Maybe she doesn't need or want the payoffs anymore. Maybe revenge is more important."

I looked at the gleaming oak barn as we approached it. Traditional in shape, the building had black doors and a matching roof with a soaring window in the front that extended from the barn doors to the peaked roof. A square cupola protruded from the roof and was topped with a weather vane. Orange daylilies sprang up from a flower bed across the front of the barn, and the soil around the blooms was dark and loose. As we got closer, I could smell the horses and the hay and even the sharp scent of manure.

"Don't drive all the way up," I said, noticing the second golf cart parked behind the barn, out of sight from the main house. "I don't want anyone to hear us coming. Aunt Connie must be down here."

Fern pulled the cart to a stop about two hundred feet from the entrance, and we all jumped off. The large sliding barn doors were closed, so I motioned for Richard and Fern to follow me as I crept around the side and peered into the windows. Richard signaled to his dog to be quiet and, surprisingly, Hermes seemed to understand as he scampered along beside us.

"I don't see them," Fern whispered to me.

I looked over my shoulder at him. "They might be in one of the stalls. We need to look in all the windows. Why did you bring the champagne?"

He held the bottle up by the neck. "Potential weapon."

Not a bad idea. I actually had no clue if Aunt Connie was packing or not. A real weapon wouldn't have been a bad idea. A better idea would have been Reese. I pulled out my phone and shot off another text telling him where we were and why. I assumed the police had arrived at the house and were preoccupying him, but I hoped he checked his phone.

"There," Richard said when he'd tiptoed ahead to the next window. "I see them. Aunt Connie looks really good for a woman who has a grown daughter."

I joined him at the window, peeking my head up high enough to glimpse inside. My mouth went dry. "That's not Aunt Connie."

CHAPTER 30

"*That's* Cara." I ducked back down so the woman with the dark bun wouldn't see me. "This doesn't make sense."

"Sure it does," Fern said, "if you assume kids always know more than parents think they do. Clearly, this kid figured out who her father was. Maybe recently, maybe a long time ago."

"Imagine how rejected she must have felt knowing her uncle was really her father but never being acknowledged by him." I bit the edge of my thumbnail. "Especially when her cousins lived such a lavish lifestyle."

"I would be bitter," Richard said. "Potentially homicidal."

I pushed myself up to get a second look. Kate and Veronica were tied up back-to-back in one of the stalls, while Cara paced in the main aisle dividing the two rows of stalls. It looked like she was talking on her phone, and I wondered if she had an accomplice.

Kate faced our window while Veronica faced Cara. I tapped lightly on the glass, hoping Cara wouldn't hear over her own phone call. Kate raised her head, and her face broke into a smile when she saw me. She used her eyes to indicate Cara behind her and shook her head. I could see Veronica trying to twist around; it looked like she was telling Kate to stop moving her head. Typical bride.

I slid back down. "Kate saw me. She and Veronica look okay. It doesn't seem like they've been hurt."

"So what do you think the cousin/sister's endgame is?" Fern asked. "They've clearly seen her, so it's not like she can get away with it. Do you think she plans on getting rid of them, or is a helicopter going to touch down in the field and take her away?"

"This isn't *Mission: Impossible*," Richard said.

"I don't know how she can get away without being stopped," I said, putting a hand up to shield my eyes from the rays of the sun as they slanted through the trees. "At this point, both Homeland Security and the police are probably on-site."

Fern put a hand to his mouth. "Do you think she's going to eliminate the witnesses?"

"No," I said, although I wasn't completely sure. "But that doesn't mean we're going to leave them there."

"There are three of us and only one of her, not counting Hermes." Richard said, extending his neck to get another look. "I spoke too soon. Here comes someone else."

We all flattened ourselves against the building as we heard a motor approaching from the path and pebbles grinding under the tires that were clearly heavier than the ones on the golf cart. Even Hermes became motionless as his tail ceased wagging and he lifted his little black nose into the air and sniffed.

Had Reese gotten my texts and commandeered a car to come join us? I heard the car brake loudly and my heart sank. Reese would never announce himself like this if he was trying to be stealthy.

I locked eyes with Richard and Fern and held a finger to my mouth as I scooted to the end of the barn, edging my head around to get a look. A shiny black Range Rover—the bride's car if I remembered correctly—had pulled up until its hood almost touched the gray double doors. I could see a figure through the tinted windows, but couldn't quite make out who it was. The driver's door opened, and a foot in shiny black dress shoes crunched down on the gravel.

I cursed to myself when I realized we'd left the golf cart sitting out in the open. So much for keeping a low profile.

"Let me see." Fern pulled me back and looked out. He turned back to us with a smile on his face. "Help has arrived."

"Really?" I wondered if Fern's idea of the cavalry was the same as mine.

Fern stepped out before I could grab him and waved his arms in the air. "Over here," he said in a stage whisper.

"What are you doing here?" It was a man's voice I knew but couldn't place.

"We're on a rescue mission," Fern said, walking forward and disappearing out of my line of sight. I cursed again and reminded myself I was going to have to review spy protocol with him after all this was over.

"Same," the man said, his voice only slightly lower than a normal speaking level. "Is Veronica inside?"

Fern must have nodded because I heard only silence.

"So who else is with you? You said 'we're on a rescue mission.'"

I motioned for Richard to stay behind, even as he shook his head in protest, and stepped out to join Fern. "Just me."

"Oh, hey Annabelle." The groom looked as surprised to see me as I was to see him. He wore his tuxedo pants and pleated-front shirt without the studs. He didn't have on his jacket or vest, and the shirt was worn without a tie, the collar spread wide.

"Hi, Tad." The moment I saw his eyes shifting toward the barn, I knew he was not here for the same reason we were. Fern must have gotten the same vibe, because he looked at me without blinking.

"We'll let you lead the way," I said. "I know you're probably eager to see your bride."

He ran a hand though his shaggy, blond hair as he approached the narrow opening in the sliding door. "Did she call you as well?"

"Did who call us?" I asked. "Cara?"

He stopped in front of the doors. "Cara? Why would Cara call me? I meant did Veronica call you?"

I looked at the blond and wondered if he was as dumb as his California surfer persona made him appear. "How could Veronica call either of us? She's being held captive."

The sliding door in front of us opened with a groan, and Cara stood in front of us, smiling and holding a small handgun. Tad backed up and bumped into Fern. Okay, so maybe I'd been wrong about him. Either that or he should become an actor pronto.

"No need for you all to stand outside and discuss me," Cara said with a wave of her arm. "Why don't you come in and join us?"

The three of us shuffled into the barn, and I couldn't help gaping as I took in how beautiful it was. Gray paving stones covered the floor in a chevron pattern, and the ceiling soared above our heads with a series of wrought iron chandeliers hanging in a row down the length of the building. The walls inside were the same polished oak as the outside, and each stall door was topped with black wrought iron latticework. I heard the soft sounds of horses moving and munching hay, and I inhaled the faint scent of cedar.

I walked until I was even with the empty stall that held Kate and Veronica. The bride faced me in her floral bathrobe with her legs straight out in front of her and crossed at the ankles.

"Are you okay?" I asked, more to Kate than to her.

The bride tossed her dark waves off her shoulder, and Kate yelped as she bumped her head. "Aside from being sore from sitting on stone all day, I'm fine."

Fern rushed over. "Well, your hair has held up beautifully. A little spray and you'll be ready to walk down the aisle."

Veronica made a face. "I'm not getting married after all this. Tad, honey, I hope you understand. Sitting here has made me realize what a huge mistake I was making."

I turned to see Tad's reaction, but he didn't seem to have one. His eyes were fixated on the gun Cara took turns pointing at us.

"That's why you called me and told me to come here but not tell anyone?" He finally found his voice. "So you could break it off?"

"Actually Cara called you and held the phone to my ear," Veronica said. "You were wonderful to me during rehab, but if I'm going to be a CEO, I need to aim higher than a hot guy who's great in bed."

I could see Kate straining to look at Tad, and I was sure this tidbit of information had moved him to the top of her possibilities list.

Fern jutted his hip out. "So there isn't going to be a wedding?"

Veronica gave him her best sad face and blew him a kiss through her bright-red lips. "Sorry, Fern. You'll still be paid of course."

"Annabelle?" Kate called to me, twisting her head in an attempt to meet my eyes. "A word please."

"You're assuming you're getting out of here in one piece," I said, stepping into the stall, the fresh hay crunching under my heels. "You do know your cousin has a gun, right?"

Veronica's high laugh echoed off the rafters. "Don't you mean my half sister?"

"Cara told you?" I asked. "That doesn't make her any less dangerous. You do know what she's done, right? Homeland Security is hauling off your father for taking some of his own nerve gas to pay off a fake ransom. Not to mention your mother's assistant is nursing a pretty big bump on her head."

Veronica pulled her hands in front of her and pushed herself to standing. "My father got what he deserved."

"Did she just pull a Houdini?" Fern stepped closer to me and grabbed my arm.

Veronica sauntered past me and stood next to Cara, leaving Kate on the ground with her hands tied behind her back and a pile of rope where the bride's hands had been. "Do you know how many women there have been over the years for him? Do you know what it's like to know your father has slept with your friends' mothers or your teachers?" She put a hand on her cousin's shoulder. "Or to discover your uncle is your father or your cousin is your sister?"

"Ohhhhhhhhhh." Fern looked between Veronica and Cara. "Now I get it."

"So you did all this to punish him," I said. "Well done. You achieved your goal. Why take my assistant?"

"That was never part of the plan," Cara said. "She wasn't supposed to come up to the room when she did, but she refused to leave."

"Even when we told her we were sneaking out for a smoke break, she insisted on coming," Veronica sighed. "Even when we pretended to want to joyride in costumes down to the barn, she refused to leave my side. You have a dedicated assistant there."

"I know," I said, pushing back the emotion that threatened to overflow into tears. "Do you mind if I untie her?"

Veronica laconically raised one shoulder, and I bent down and began unwinding the ropes around Kate's wrists. Her forehead was sweaty, and strands of blond hair stuck to the sides of her face, but otherwise her bob was still bouncy and her eye makeup still flawless. If I wasn't so happy to see her, I'd have to hate her.

"Did you know?" I whispered.

"Not for sure until just now." Kate rubbed her wrists when I'd freed them. "The joyriding in costumes and masks was weird, but I thought the bride needed to blow off some steam. I tried to text you where we were going, but I must have dropped my phone. I did think Veronica was acting pretty calm throughout the entire ordeal considering what a high-maintenance pain in the neck she'd been during the planning. What's this about a nerve agent?"

I hoisted her to a standing position and put an arm around her waist. "I'll tell you later."

"So your dad goes to jail, and I go home and, what?" the groom asked. "You become the new CEO and ride off into the spoiled-little-rich-girl sunset?"

Veronica's nostrils flared. "Don't be difficult, Tad. You've had a nice run of it. Let's not ruin it now."

"Ruin it now?" he yelled. "You faked your own kidnapping, and now you're dumping me on our wedding day. How am I the one ruining it?"

"He makes an excellent point," Fern said.

Cara rolled her eyes and fired a shot at Tad. "I hate lovers' spats."

Fern screamed as Tad clutched the top of his arm where red had begun to seep through his shirt. The groom glanced down at the blood and began to sway in place. Before he hit the floor, Kate ran over and caught him under one arm, and Fern took him by the other, and they lowered him to the floor.

"You shot him?" Veronica and I said at the same time.

"You didn't want to?" Cara asked her cousin. "Come on. We talked about this. You can do better than him."

Veronica stared down at her former fiancé as Kate pressed both hands to his wound and blood stained the gray paving stones beneath him.

"He's not dead." Cara let out an exasperated breath. "I haven't killed anyone."

"Yet," I said, and her eyes flicked to me. "You must have thought about what happens next, right? I mean, you're the brains behind this, am I right?"

Cara pressed her lips together, but Veronica fluttered a hand at me. "No one needs to get hurt. There's plenty of money to go around now that my father is out of the picture and I'm in charge."

"You think you're going to pay us off?" I asked. "All of us?"

"How much were you thinking?" Fern asked, looking up from the floor.

I shot him a look.

"What?" He looked abashed. "It never hurts to ask."

"Listen to your friend." Cara waved her gun in Fern's direction. "That is, unless wedding planners make a lot more than I think they do."

I'd never admit that wedding planning wasn't always the most lucrative business considering the number of hours we had to put in to pull off big weddings. And we couldn't exactly charge clients more for being high-maintenance, although I often wished we could have a list of surcharges for things like calling more than twice a day, sending over a hundred emails a week all about lipstick colors, or texting me after midnight.

"I'm sure Annabelle and her friends will see reason." Veronica winked at me. "After all, my mother did pay them all a pretty penny to plan my wedding."

I felt a surge of irritation that Veronica thought I would help her cover up a crime just because I was her wedding planner. This definitely did not fall under my job description.

"Of course she did," Cara said. "You are the princess, after all."

Veronica's cheeks became mottled red. "What does that mean?"

As the two women bickered, I heard Kate's voice.

"Annabelle, I think he's losing a lot of blood."

I could smell the metallic tang and tried not to focus on the bright red covering her hands. We had to get Tad out of here and to the hospital. This wedding day may have been a disaster and would be my first without an actual wedding ceremony, but I was not going to let the groom bleed out in the barn. I slipped my hand into my dress pocket as subtly as I could and tried to dial 9-1-1 without seeing the screen.

I heard the sound of tires on gravel and stopped tapping on my phone. All our heads swiveled toward the open barn doors as one of the black-clad security guards entered with his gun drawn.

I let out a breath. "Thank heavens. I was beginning to wonder what you guys were here for."

The guy was young with brown hair cut short and sunglasses he now pushed onto the top of his head. His eyes scanned the group, dipping to the groom splayed out on the ground, and landing on Cara. He lowered his gun. "You said no one would get hurt."

It took me a moment to process what happened. "Hold on," I said. "You're with her? You're part of this?"

Cara sauntered over to the guard and flung an arm around him, her gun still pointed in our general direction. "I've been spending a lot of time at the house and so has Mason. One thing led to another."

He tucked his gun behind him in the waistband of his pants. "You said this was just to teach your father a lesson."

"It is, baby," Cara cooed at him. "This was an accident."

Fern rolled his eyes. "Please tell me all straight men are not this gullible."

"This explains why the security team didn't see anything and why the barn was never checked," I said, more to myself than to anyone else.

"We need to get out of here," the guard said to Cara. "The house is crawling with cops and Homeland Security. I have my SUV waiting at the far end of the property line like you said. We can be there in five minutes in the golf cart."

Cara grinned. "And my father?"

"Dragged off in handcuffs."

Veronica flinched and a look of regret crossed her face. "I should go tell the rest of my family I'm okay."

"Hands up." Daniel's booming voice caused everyone in the barn to freeze as he and his brother rushed in with guns drawn.

We all lifted our arms except for Kate, who kept her hands pressed to the groom's gunshot wound. Cara dropped her gun, and Daniel lifted Mason's out of his pants before he could reach for it. He kicked both off to the side, ordering the couple to put their hands on their heads. Mike spun Veronica around and began to cuff her.

"What are you doing?" She tried to shake his hands off. "I'm one of the victims."

"Nice try, princess," he said. "I heard everything."

"And I recorded it." Fern produced his phone from the pocket of his black pants.

Richard hurried into the center aisle of the barn, his eyes going to the groom and his usually tan face paling. "Are we too late?"

Hermes ran over and sniffed around the groom's head before giving him a quick lick and settling himself beside Kate.

"When did Hermes get here?" Kate asked.

"It's a bit complicated," I said, "but basically Leatrice is here dressed as a jester and may or may not be romantically involved with Sidney Allen."

Kate shook her head. "How long have I been in this barn?"

Veronica started to cry as Daniel led her and her cousin outside. Through the open barn doors, I could hear sirens in the distance getting closer.

Mike came to stand beside me, his eyes going to the groom. "I called an ambulance. They should be here in a few minutes." He put a hand to my waist. "Are you okay?"

"Kate's okay. I'm okay. I take it you got my texts?"

The corners of his mouth twitched up. "Actually, Richard found me and told me everything."

"He found you?" I asked, watching my best friend kneel next to Kate and give her a one-armed hug.

"Actually, he almost mowed me down in that golf cart, but yeah, he found me and told me and my brother we had to come with him immediately—no questions asked." Reese rubbed a hand over his forehead. "Riding with him down here while he steered with one hand and held his dog with the other might have been the scariest two minutes of my life. He filled us in on everything so rapidly he might want to consider moonlighting as an auctioneer."

I put a hand to my mouth to keep from laughing and crying at the same time. "That sounds like Richard." I craned myself to look out the barn doors. "How did we not hear the golf cart drive up?"

"We off-roaded on the grass for the last half of the ride and parked a decent distance away."

"Good thinking," I said.

Reese flicked his eyes to Richard. "You should thank Mario Andretti."

Richard stood up and joined us. "Nice work, Detective."

Mike held out his hand. "You too. This never would have happened without your quick thinking and even quicker driving."

Richard cleared his throat and shook my boyfriend's hand as patches of pink appeared on his cheeks.

Maybe this day wasn't a total loss after all.

CHAPTER 31

"*A*re you sure about this?" I asked Alexandra as she wheeled the wedding cake to the center of the dinner tent dance floor and Hermes trotted along behind her.

I had to raise my voice over the clattering and clunking of the band packing up and the waiters clearing the tables of all china and crystal. The tall floral arrangements had been removed and lined up to one side of the tent, and one of Buster and Mack's white delivery vans had backed up with its milk truck back doors open so their setup team could load them inside to be delivered to local retirement homes. Cardboard boxes had been filled with Venetian masks wrapped in bubble wrap and were now stacked on the edge of the dance floor where men on tall ladders stood pulling down the fabric draping the inside of the tent ceiling.

"It's the only food that hasn't been tainted," she said, holding up the silver cake knife the bride and groom would have used to cut their ceremonial first slice. "And I, for one, am starving."

"More bubbly anyone?" Fern asked, holding up the bottle he hadn't needed to use down at the barn before topping off his own glass.

"You don't all have to stay," I said for at least the tenth time as I leaned my elbows against the bare plywood of a table that had been stripped of its tablecloth. Part of the Wedding Belles service was to stay until the end of break-down, and after such a long and emotionally draining day, I was rethinking that part of our contract. I wondered how strange it would be to add a clause about weddings being canceled by criminal activity or the bride being hauled off to jail.

"So you've said." Fern winked from across the table where he sat in a gold ladder-backed chair next to Leatrice.

"I'm here for the cake," Sidney Allen said while making googly eyes at Leatrice.

His performers had all packed up the moment they'd heard the wedding was off and had left as soon as they'd given their statements to the police. I'd hoped Sidney Allen would join them in the mass exodus, but he and Leatrice now seemed to be attached at the hip, although his pants were hiked up much higher than that, and her hips were still bedecked with bells.

Kate nudged me as she looked at Leatrice and Sidney Allen whispering and giggling. "Am I losing my mind, or did Leatrice snag herself a boyfriend faster than even I could?"

"Let's not use the term 'boyfriend,'" I said. I was hoping this was a passing infatuation. I still couldn't wrap my head around the idea of being charmed by Sidney Allen, but I had to admit he was more palatable when he wasn't screaming into his headset and running around flapping his arms about his creative vision.

"I don't know." Kate tilted her head as she watched Sidney hitch his pants almost to his armpits and slip an arm around Leatrice. "They're kind of cute together."

"Did you hit your head?" I asked her. "Should we have you tested for a concussion?"

She smiled at me and took a sip of her champagne. "Today gave me a new appreciation for the small things in life."

Richard leaned over me from his seat on the other side of me.

"Sidney Allen and Leatrice definitely qualify as small things." He dropped his voice even lower. "Pretty soon he's going to be a head resting on top of his pants."

I swatted at him. "Be nice."

"When am I not nice?" Richard asked, feigning an expression of being deeply wounded as Hermes leapt into his lap. "Do *not* answer," he said as Kate and I both opened our mouths.

I patted him on the leg and rubbed his dog's head. "I'm actually proud of how well you're handling this. You had to throw out all the food you'd prepared for the wedding, and you didn't swoon once."

"Swoon?" Richard wrinkled his nose at me. "Honestly, Annabelle. As if I swoon."

Off the top of my head, I could think of multiple occasions where Richard had fainted from the stress of an event or murder investigation. I decided not to argue with him since he'd been the one to call in the cavalry for us today, and he was handling everything remarkably well.

"It helps that we were paid in advance," Mack said as he walked up with Buster behind him. "None of us would be nearly so calm if we were out of pocket for all of this."

"So true." Fern hiccupped. "Although I'm guessing we won't get tipped today."

Since the father of the bride had been taken in for questioning by Homeland Security; the bride and her cousin had been arrested for multiple counts of kidnapping, obstructing an investigation, and attempted murder; and the bride's former fiancé was in surgery to remove a bullet from his shoulder, it felt safe to say that tipping was the last thing on the mother of the bride's mind. I'd been a bit surprised she hadn't fallen to pieces when she'd seen her daughter in handcuffs like Aunt Connie had when she'd seen Cara. Mrs. Hamilton had become deathly calm when she learned her daughter had been involved in staging her own kidnapping to ruin her father, declining to follow her to the police station and instead going with the bride's brother to the hospital to check on Sherry and the groom.

"The really wealthy ones never tip well," Kate said. "And sometimes clients tip every single person except the planners, when we're the ones who found all the vendors for them and made it possible for the rest of the team to do such a good job."

"Cake bakers never get tipped at all." Alexandra put a pair of cake plates with slices of wedding cake on them in the middle of the table.

"Because you aren't usually here at the bitter end," I said.

"Maybe I should become a cake designer," Richard said, passing a cake plate to Kate before giving one to me. "You get to drop off the cake and go home. No late nights. No on-site drama."

"Who are you kidding?" I said. "You love all the excitement of a wedding day. You'd go out of your mind if you had to stay at home and wonder if they liked your cake or not."

Richard tapped his fingers against the rough wood of the table. "I never thought about that. Never mind."

I took a bite of the pale-pink cake layered with a dark-pink filling. I'd forgotten the flavors the couple had chosen since we'd booked the cake so long ago, but as soon as I bit in, I recognized the pink champagne cake topped with raspberry mousse. The cake was a moist genoise and the tartness of the fluffy mousse balanced its sweetness.

"Forget food," Fern said as he tasted the cake. "This is all I need in life. Cake and champagne."

"There's champagne in the cake," Alexandra told him as she cut more pieces.

Fern rolled his eyes into the back of his head as he chewed. "Even better."

"How are things in the house?" I asked Buster and Mack since they'd come from inside.

"Deserted." Buster pulled a chair over to our table and it groaned as he sat on it. "The family is either at the police station or the hospital, and it looks like the cops are almost done taking statements in the kitchen."

We'd all given our statements first since we were directly involved in the case, Kate's testimony being the most damning to Cara since she was the one witness to how the cousins/sisters colluded.

"So the gummy bear I found on the floor really wasn't a clue?" I asked.

"Sorry. I must have dropped it by accident. Same with my phone. I think it fell out of my dress pocket when I pulled that costume over my head."

"That explains the white feather I found outside the front door," I said. "Veronica must have intentionally kicked her phone under the bed before you three left. That way we couldn't track her."

"I should have thought it was odd to wear costumes to ride down to the barn for a smoke break, but the bride seemed so freaked out about getting married and kept saying she wanted to do something wild." Kate wiped her mouth with a black paper napkin with "Veronica and Tad" stamped on it in gold ink. "She was desperate to sneak a cigarette but said her mother would freak out if she caught her. Apparently Veronica smokes in the barn pretty regularly."

"And her mother has no idea?" I asked. "Is there anything this family tells the truth about?"

"Doubtful." Richard produced a dog treat from inside his jacket pocket and gave it to an eager Hermes. "Mark my words. The rot comes from the top."

I tended to agree with him. The parents had set the example of deception from the beginning, and it had filtered down throughout the family.

"So who drove the golf cart?" I asked

"Cara. I rode in the back. I planned on texting you on the way, but I realized I'd dropped my phone. By the time my Spidey sense was really tingling, we were inside the barn and Cara had a gun on us. Veronica played along with it up until the end though. I wish now she hadn't. I had to hear her whine all day about her ruined wedding when she was behind it the whole time."

"I wonder when they hatched this plan." I took a sip of champagne even though it was no longer cold.

"Almost six months ago." Reese took long steps toward us, brushing an errant curl off his forehead. Daniel followed behind and both men looked wiped out. "According to the bride, the grandmother told Cara and started planting the idea of getting revenge on Mr. Hamilton for the past two years. Cara finally told Veronica they were sisters when she visited her in rehab, but it wasn't until halfway through the wedding planning she suggested they get back at their father."

"So that dried up old granny was behind it all?" Fern made a face. "I never liked her. Mark my words, you can never trust someone with a perm that tight."

Mack nodded his agreement. "I wonder what Mrs. Hamilton and Aunt Connie think since she's the reason their daughters will be going to prison."

"I did hear the bride's mother scream something about taking her house away," Daniel said. "And the old lady may be facing criminal conspiracy charges of her own."

"Good," Buster said, his voice a rumble. "She should reap what she sowed."

"Speaking of karma," Reese added. "Tina Pink was also slapped with enough criminal charges to send her away for quite a while."

"Whose idea was it to ruin the wedding day?" I asked. "That's who I want to kill."

"Get in line," Kate said.

I immediately felt a pang of guilt. Even though all of us had been stressed out and worried, Kate had been the one to spend her day tied to a bridezilla, not knowing what was going on or what would happen to her. "Are you sure you're okay?" I leaned over to her and asked in a quiet voice.

"I'm fine." She gave me a sly smile. "All in a day's work, right? I wouldn't be averse to discussing hazard pay though."

Reese rested his hands on my shoulders. "Does today mean I'm officially on your payroll now?"

Richard handed a piece of cake over his head to Reese. "I do believe you were working for me when this day began, although if you wish to continue as a sommelier, we have a considerable amount of work to do."

Kate raised an eyebrow and mouthed "sommelier?" to me.

"I think I'll stick to detective work." Reese eyed the pink cake. "But if I ever need a wheelman, I know who to call."

"Yes, well." Richard didn't look at Reese, but I could tell he was pleased with the compliment.

Daniel took the seat next to Kate. "It looks like your quick thinking might have saved the groom. He lost blood, but not as much as he would have if you hadn't kept pressure on the wound."

Kate looked down at her hands, even though we'd washed all the blood off them. "I hope he's okay. No one should be dumped on their wedding day and then shot. Talk about adding insult to inquiry."

"Something like that," Richard muttered, although I knew he'd actually missed Kate's mangled expressions.

Kate put a hand on Daniel's leg. "Thank you for coming in with guns blazing to save the day. You were quite the hero."

"Anytime," Daniel said.

She angled her body closer to his, and her dress crept up higher on her bare thigh. "Maybe I could thank you properly over dinner."

Daniel's face flushed. "It would be my pleasure."

Leatrice clapped her hands and her outfit jingled. "We could double date." She looked over at me and at Reese standing behind me. "Or triple date even."

"Better you than me," Richard said from behind one hand.

I looked around the table at the weary yet happy faces surrounding me: Mack and Buster on their second pieces of cake, Alexandra happily cutting up her creation for us to enjoy, Leatrice and Sidney Allen making eyes at each other, Fern popping the cork on another champagne bottle, Richard feeding Hermes little bits of icing when he thought I wasn't looking, Kate flirting with Daniel Reese, and Daniel getting flustered by the attention. I put a hand over Reese's hand on my shoulder and looked up at him.

He leaned down close to my ear. "I'd rather go on a double date with Richard and Hermes."

"That can be arranged," Richard said without looking at either of us.

I laughed, noticing the upturned edges of Richard's mouth. I had plenty of time to figure out how to wiggle my way out of a date with Leatrice and Sidney Allen. At the moment, I wanted to savor time with my friends doing what we loved to do—drinking champagne, teasing each other, and congratulating ourselves on surviving yet another wedding.

FREE DOWNLOAD!

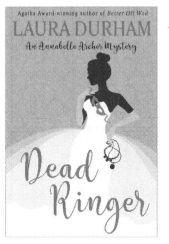

ALSO BY LAURA DURHAM

Read the entire Annabelle Archer Series in order:

Better Off Wed

For Better Or Hearse

Dead Ringer

Review To A Kill

Death On The Aisle

Night of the Living Wed

Eat, Prey, Love

Groomed For Murder

Wed or Alive

To Love and To Perish

To get notices whenever I release a new book, follow me on BookBub:

https://www.bookbub.com/profile/laura-durham

Did you enjoy this book? You can make a big difference!

I'm extremely lucky to have a loyal bunch of readers, and honest reviews are the best way to help bring my books to the attention of new readers.

If you enjoyed *Wed or Alive*, I would be forever grateful if you could spend two minutes leaving a review (it can be as short as you like) on Goodreads, Bookbub, or your favorite retailer.

Thanks for reading and reviewing!

This book is dedicated to all the photographers, florists, caterers, hair stylists, makeup artists, band members, DJs, lighting guys, and videographers I spent almost every weekend with for the better part of two decades. There are too many to name, but you know who you are. Thank you for the friendships forged in the trenches (and for making a tough job fun)!

ACKNOWLEDGMENTS

A huge thank you to all of my wonderful readers, especially my beta readers and my review team. You are all eagle-eyed wizards! A special shout-out to the beta readers who catch all my goofs and let me know if something doesn't make sense before the book goes to print: Linda Reachill, Sheila Kraemer, Jan Scholefield, Linda Fore, Annemarie Esposito, Wendy Green, Vivian Shane, Charlene Eshleman, Sandra Anderson, Katherine Munro, Sharon Thach, Tony Noice, Barb Foerst, Karen Diamond, Lisa Hudson, Nicole Drake, Tricia Knox, Patricia Joyner, Carol Spayde, Regina Davis-Sowers, Claire Matturo, and Bill Saunders. You are incredible!

A heartfelt thank you to everyone who leaves reviews. They really make a difference, and I am grateful for every one of them!

Thank you to my ever-supportive and extremely patient husband and children. Living with a writer isn't always easy. I love you!

ABOUT THE AUTHOR

Laura Durham has been writing for as long as she can remember and has been plotting murders since she began planning weddings over twenty years ago in Washington, DC. Her first novel, BETTER OFF WED, won the Agatha Award for Best First Novel.

When she isn't writing or wrangling brides, Laura loves traveling with her family, standup paddling, perfecting the perfect brownie recipe, and reading obsessively.

She loves hearing from readers and she would love to hear from you! Send an email or connect on Facebook, Instagram, or Twitter (click the icons below).

Find me on:
www.lauradurham.com
laura@lauradurham.com

 facebook.com/authorlauradurham
twitter.com/reallauradurham
instagram.com/lauradurhamauthor

Made in the USA
Middletown, DE
20 September 2018